The Murder Knight

Anuj R. Malhotra

Printed in India

IndiePress

ISBN: 978-93-6045-213-1

First Printing, 2024

Indie Press

A division of Nasadiya Technologies Private Ltd.

Koramangala, Bengaluru

Karnataka-560029

http://indiepress.in/

Edited by Literary Connect

Typeset by MAP Systems, Bengaluru

Book Cover designed by Sankhasubhro Nath

Publishing Consultant: Samyuktha Prasanan

Thank you for all your blessings and guidance.
Miss you immensely ma.

(12.10.1947 - 27.12.2022)

Contents

Chapter 1

The Crime Scene

On a bright Monday morning, Charles Knight, a detective with the police, parked his car and walked out with his coffee in hand. He entered the station and was greeted by the deputies as he made his way to his desk. There, he found files of cases being investigated by him, the red flags indicating the notorious ones. Two pictures sat on the side of his table: the first, a small formal family portrait, and the other, a quirky one with the love of his life, Lisa.

Charles stared at the family picture for a few seconds, sipping his latte. He looked at each person individually: Robert, his father, a ruthless lawyer in court but the most loving person outside of it; his late mother, who died of a severe illness; and his sister Darcy, a strong, independent businesswoman. With a smile, he said, "Good morning, family," as he started his day by going through one of the files on his table.

A deputy approached his desk, saying, "The day starts early, detective. We already have a call for a homicide. The victim was shot point-blank. We are heading out there now. Do you want to come along, or should we go ahead?"

Charles took the papers. "You guys go ahead and secure the crime scene. I'll catch up." The deputy placed a small piece of paper with the address on the table and left.

Charles continued with his work, not even looking at the address as he went about his morning routine. After a while, his mobile phone rang. It was Darcy. He smiled because he always requested that she not call in the morning, but his pesky sister loved to trouble him. He picked up the call and joked, "What did I say about morning peacetime, Darcy?"

"He is dead, Charles... He... (sobs)... has been shot! Please, just come quickly," said Darcy hysterically, her voice trembling.

"Shot? Who? What do you mean? Who has been shot? Why are you crying? You're not making any sense, Darcy. Darcy, are you there? Are you okay?"

"Father, he has been shot. Come quick, please, just come quickly!" continued Darcy, crying and shaking. Charles glanced at the piece of paper left by his deputy. It was the address of his family mansion. His heart skipped a beat, and he froze in shock.

Realising he had to act swiftly, Charles snapped out of it and rushed to the mansion. "Cancel my calendar for the day. Something urgent has come up, and I need to be there."

"But the captain is on his way to meet you!" shouted Kim from behind as Charles ran out.

Charles drove off to the countryside, towards the family mansion. As he sped with the sirens blaring, the events of last night started playing in his head. Just last night, they were all at the mansion for dinner, laughing, joking, and making fun of each other. Their father, Robert, shared embarrassing anecdotes of Charles and Darcy's childhood with Lisa.

Charles kept calling Darcy on the way to the mansion, but there was no response. He was worried for her. He had never heard her speak in such a trembling and shaky voice—the confident and strong character she always had, thought Charles. "Come on, Darcy, pick up the damn phone!" shouted Charles as he hit the steering wheel with his palms, wishing all of this was not true.

Charles reached the mansion and drove up the driveway. The entire driveway was full of police cars and other teams, a mix of red and blue lights, with a dozen deputies standing there, cordoning off the area. As Charles got out of his car, he knew his worst fear had come true.

Just on the verge of breaking down and hanging on by a thread, Charles mustered up the courage to go inside.

"You are not allowed to be here," said the deputy, stopping Charles since he was not in uniform. Charles showed his detective badge. "What is the situation?" he asked in a weak tone, yet he was trying to be strong.

"There has been a murder on-site. The victim was shot at point-blank range. Only one casualty. The shooter is yet to be caught. We have been asked to set up a perimeter. No one is in or out," said the officer.

Charles climbed the three steps on the front porch, shivering, shocked, and sweating. He knew this was real now: his father was shot dead. He pushed the main door to enter the common room.

Darcy was in the corner of the room. She saw Charles and broke down. She walked towards him, crying, "Thank God you came. He is dead, Charles. (sobbing) He has been shot!"

At this point, Charles could no longer stop himself. He broke down as he tightly hugged Darcy. "But how? We were all here just last night, he was fine. I can't believe it. I can't... I just..."

Charles kept hugging Darcy as they both tried to console each other.

"I was in my room when it happened, doing my meetings. Andy came up running. I'd never seen him so hysterical. I rushed down with him in a panic. I saw him in a pool of blood and just shattered. I was numb," said Darcy, sobbing and choking. "I called you as soon as I came to my senses."

A deputy walked up to Charles and asked both of them to follow him. Charles and Darcy gathered themselves and followed him slowly to their father's study, where he was shot.

"This could come as a shock to you both, seeing him in such a state. I sympathise with your loss, but please, brace yourself," said the deputy escorting them.

They opened the door and entered his study. The teams working there stood aside for them.

There he was, lying on the table, on the side of his face, in front of his computer. His eyes were still half open, his body lifeless, and blood was all over the desk and on the floor. A few drops near the table formed a line going to the centre of the study. A single shot to the heart, his shirt red and black. The blood had thickened and turned black around the outlines.

His computer was still on, and one hand was on the keyboard. His other hand was clenched, near the family picture that he was facing when he passed. The picture was an exact replica of the one Charles had on his table. A book was kept open on the side of the table, with a page marked as if he were reading it.

There was an empty bullet shell on the floor, in the centre of the room, where the blood drops ended. The killer must have shot him from here. The bullet was marked by the forensic team with a flag to store it as evidence later.

As Charles saw this, he just stood there like a zombie. Time froze, all sounds and chatter seemed muted, and the lights seemed dim. All he could see was his father lying there, lifeless. Tears rolled down his cheeks. There was love and respect in his eyes for such a strong, towering figure. He had never had such a reaction to a lifeless body in his years of work as a police detective.

Darcy sobbed, "No, father, no, no, you can't leave us. No, you are our strength. You are our life. You are our bond. Not after mom, no, no." A daughter's love and affection for her father took over. She sprang towards him. Just as she grabbed his hand on the table, a deputy shouted, "Stop her!!!"

The other police personnel at the scene closed in to pull her back. They grabbed her by the shoulder, but not before she could hold her father one last time. His face was lifeless and as cold as ice. The desire of a daughter to hold her father for the last time was short-lived as the deputies pulled her back.

"Ma'am, please get a grip on yourself," said the deputy with a stern tone. "This is still an active crime scene, and you are contaminating evidence by touching the victim." Darcy agreed and stepped back, wiping her tears with her handkerchief.

Charles, who had been standing there expressionless, taking it all in, came to his senses when he heard this. "The victim!" shouted Charles at the top of his voice, his face red with anger. "That victim is my father, and his name was Robert Knight."

Charles grabbed Darcy's hand and pulled her to him. "We need to get through this together. We need to be strong. We have to accept that our father is no longer with us," said Charles in a shaky and weak tone.

"But Charles, who could have done this? He was such a loving and caring person. You have to solve this. Promise me, please promise me," pleaded Darcy as she wiped her tears.

"I will, Darcy, but one step at a time. For now, we need to get through the current situation. I am still trying to make sense of it all. After mom, he was the only one we had. He was the family's strength. But I don't understand who could have shot him. He was always so helpful to everyone."

Charles' phone rang. Captain Nate was calling. "I heard about your father, Charles. I am deeply saddened. Please accept my condolences. If you or Darcy require anything from me, do let me know. You have my full support."

"I do, Captain. I just need one small thing from you. I want to take the lead on this case."

"You know I cannot allow that, Charles. You have a personal interest, which might hamper your judgement in the matter. Would you be emotionally stable enough to handle this investigation properly? Going through every detail again and again?"

"Yes, I would," said Charles, with a hint of anger and certainty in his voice.

"But he is your father. You are connected to the victim. You cannot be a judge in your own case."

"Captain, please make it happen. I know you can. I have never asked you for anything like this in my years of service. Please, I beg you!"

"Fine, you don't have to beg, Charles. I will take over the investigation in my name. That way, you can investigate on the side and have access to all the information. I will call the detective on-site. But remember, Charles is only on the side. If I see you making one decision out of emotion and not logic, you are out." Nate cut the call.

Being in charge now, Charles walked up to his father's body. While examining it, he just couldn't hold back his tears.

Before something was missed, work had to be done, and evidence had to be collected. Cameras clicked photos from every angle, with flashes of light and evidence markings everywhere.

"He was facing the family picture when he passed," said Darcy, her voice trembling.

"He was a loving father, Darcy, always putting us before anyone else," replied Charles as he stepped back from the body. "But I don't understand one thing. Why did he not make a run for it or try to protect himself? It's as if he just sat there waiting to be shot at. There seems to be no sign of struggle, nothing out of place, no weapons found, nothing!"

Charles paused for a second, his attention drawn to something shiny lying under the table next to his father's shoe. He asked for an evidence bag and picked it up. "It's a cufflink."

Immediately, Charles checked the cufflinks worn by his father. They were identical, but both were on his sleeve. Three cufflinks of the same kind. He thought to himself, "Where is the fourth one from the other pair?" He looked around the table but found nothing.

"I remember these. He had them made for the family and his firm, even for gifts, right, Darcy?"

Darcy took a closer look and said, "Yeah, you are right. I had a pair too. I wore them out long ago, so I stopped using them."

"So, assuming this belongs to the killer, we have more than a dozen suspects now. However, who could have scorned him so badly that they killed him? There are too many variables at this point."

Charles looked around the room and spotted the camera installed there. He immediately signalled for a deputy to come to him. "Get the camera footage," said Charles, pointing towards the camera at the top right corner of the study.

While the deputy left to get the footage, Charles kept looking around the bookshelves and in the corners to find something of worth.

The officer came back after some time. "It's gone. The hard drive is missing for this camera," he said, pointing at it.

"What?" retorted Charles, shocked. "How can that be? How can the drive be missing?"

"There are five DVRs installed for all the cameras in the vicinity. This camera on the inside of the study you see there has a separate DVR and the drive from this particular one is missing."

"What? How the hell can it be gone? How long had the killer been here? How did the killer know where the drive was?"

"We have extracted the footage from the outside camera. Would you like to see that?"

"Does it have anything useful?"

"Yes, it does."

"Show me."

The deputy handed him a screen. "There is no audio either."

"This just keeps getting better, doesn't it?" said Charles, frustrated.

Charles and Darcy leaned in to see the screen, scared and fearful in their eyes. It was not easy seeing their own father get shot.

The footage was a bit distant but quite clear. They slowly pressed play.

"So there he is, sitting on the computer," pointed out Charles. It was surprising, given his father's orthodox nature and how miserable he was when it came to technology. He loved his pen and paper to the extent that he still carried a pocket phone book. "It looks like he is typing something."

In the video, Robert was seen on the computer and then turning around to talk to someone. Robert didn't seem to be agitated at all, considering he was about to be shot by someone.

"Who is he talking to?" asked Darcy with anticipation in her eyes. "This could very well solve the murder right now."

"It looks like he is arguing with someone now, and it's getting heated."

"But with whom?" exclaimed Charles with anger. "The angle of the camera is such that the entry wall is blocking the other side, and the person is not stepping out from behind the wall."

Robert was seen arguing fiercely with someone, his face red and his arms moving around as if to make a point, pointing at the person opposite him several times. Then Robert was seen returning to his computer.

After a few seconds, Robert was again seen getting up from his chair and walking towards the other side of the room. His face appeared a bit calmer, his hands as if trying to explain something and not the angry gestures he had before. It looked as if he was trying to pacify the mystery person on the other side.

All of a sudden, Robert put his hands up slightly and started stepping back. An arm of the other person holding a gun was visible, wearing a black suit, a white shirt, and a brown glove. Robert stood with his hand slightly up, his face now turning stern and straight, as if accepting the inevitable, as if he knew his end was near.

Suddenly, Robert pounced towards the person with the gun, trying to grab his hand and pull him toward his computer. The other person managed to get his hand free, but a cufflink was torn from the sleeve of the killer's shirt by Robert during the scuffle. Then there was a flash of light, and everyone knew what it was, even without audio.

"Oh, God!" said Darcy, covering her face with her hands as she broke down again. Sadness and helplessness could be seen in Charles' eyes as he held Darcy. He kept looking at the footage.

Robert was covered in blood now, with the bullet in his chest. He walked weakly to his computer, his legs trembling, the light of life slowly dwindling away from his eyes. He grabbed the chair and pulled himself onto it. He was seen typing something and trying to reach for the photo on the table, his body giving way due to blood loss. He then stopped moving completely.

Charles asked the deputy showing the footage, "Can you rewind the footage a bit, keep going... more... there, do you see? When father grabbed the other person's arm, he ripped this cufflink off, the one we found under the table."

"Yes, you are right," she sobbed, wiping her tears and pointing to the screen.

"Run this cufflink for fingerprint analysis immediately. We need to know who the killer was before he escapes the country and check the footage from other cameras as well. Maybe there's something there."

Charles walked back to the computer where Robert was seen typing something. He leaned closer to the computer screen and spotted a minimised tab below. He clicked on the tab to maximise it. To his surprise, it was an email addressed to him.

"An email! He knew how to write them." Charles then wondered, why would he write an email when he was shot instead of calling for help or running.

"He had recently started, you know, because of all the pressure from his firm to reply to the confidential emails addressed to him from the clients. He really struggled with it, but for the sake of his clients, he learned it," said Darcy.

The email just had the words "FA" written on it.

"That means nothing," said Charles.

"It could be nothing, but it could also be that he was trying to say something. It could be the initials of a person, maybe the person who shot him."

"You could be right, but why write when you are about to die? That's the question I can't seem to get my head around."

"You know how he was, Charles, always with his little mysteries and his love for hiding things, asking us to scout for them when we were kids."

While talking to Darcy, Charles saw the book rack shake just a bit behind her.

"There's someone hiding behind the book rack," whispered Charles as he moved to it, signalling for the deputies to cover him and be ready.

He quickly took his gun out and signalled the deputy to move forward and cover him. With a finger to his lips, he gestured to Darcy and everyone to be quiet and to step back to a safe distance. He slowly moved to the book rack.

The deputy went around the corner, and everyone heard him saying, "Don't try to run, hands where I can see them. If you have any arms, please place them on the floor." The deputy then grabbed the arm of the person to pull him out. A person wearing a black suit came out from behind the shelf.

"Andy!" said Charles.

"Master Charles, please help me! I did not do anything."

"You know him?" asked the deputy.

"Yes, he's my father's butler."

"Then why were you hiding behind the bookshelf?" asked Charles with a suspicious tone.

"I wasn't hiding. I was just seeing what was happening from a safe distance. I came back from the kitchen, and the room was full of officers. They asked me to stay in the kitchen. I did not want to cause any hindrance while they were gathering evidence."

"What happened here, Andy?"

"I got a bit worried when Master Robert did not call me after his meeting. I heard a low bang but did not pay much attention to it. When Master Robert did not ring for me, even after half an hour, I got a little suspicious and decided to check. I came to the room, and Master Robert was there, lying on the table with blood all over. I froze. I could not move."

"When I gathered myself from the shock of seeing Master Robert like that, I called the police station and called Miss Darcy from her room. I could not make sense of what had happened. I went blank. Miss Darcy then called you, which I should have also done."

"When I saw red and blue lights outside the window, I thought that they would suspect me of being involved since I was the one who discovered the body. I calmed down a bit, knowing you would come with the officers since Miss Darcy called you. To my surprise, you were not there with them. So I decided it was best to keep my distance and wait for you, Charles. I knew you would come sooner or later."

"It's understandable, Andy, but you were in the house when the shot was fired, so you have to give your statement to the police and come in for standard questioning. You have nothing to worry about."

"I will, Master Charles. I am innocent. I was with Master Robert for the past 30 years. I could never think of doing this. I will cooperate fully," said Andy in a stammering voice.

"It's alright, Andy."

Charles turned to the deputy and said, "Andy has been in the family for the past 30 years. Keep that in mind when you question him and take his statement."

The officer nodded in agreement.

During the course of the night, evidence was collected and bagged, with cameras clicking from all angles. Charles and Darcy stood on the side, watching. The body of their father was carefully moved to a body bag kept on the side for him. A number was being assigned to him, like any other body found at a crime scene. The body bag was then kept aside for the postmortem later. The forensics experts were doing their jobs, and the blood spatter expert was conducting his analysis on one side, while the fingerprint experts were on the other side dusting the bookshelves for prints. Charles just stood there—a bit sad, helpless, and also angered at the same time.

"I just wish there was some way, some manner, I could have helped him, could have saved him. Maybe if I had stayed back last night after dinner and hadn't gone back home, leaving him alone here!"

"How could you have known this would happen, Charles?"

"There has to be something else, something we are missing."

Robert's body was wheeled out of the room in the body bag and into an ambulance for the postmortem.

"I think it's best for everyone if we stay here for the night, Charles. The day has been an emotional turmoil, and I am too tired to go back home."

"I agree. I don't want to be alone today. It's just us now, just us."

"Back to our old rooms, I guess, just like the old days. Father would always come to check on us and tuck us in, remember? He would always go to your room first, Darcy, then come to mine."

"Well, it was the exact opposite with you and mom. She would spend hours with you. We never realised it at that time, but they did have a way to balance things out. Father was always so full of life around her. After mom, he just kept mostly to himself and to his work. It was as if he had lost everything."

"Let's just rest. My mind is numb, my body is giving up. I just can't stand anymore," said Charles.

Charles climbed the spiral staircase up to his room, and Darcy followed a few steps behind him. Charles seemed lost and walked like a person dragging himself, deep in his thoughts.

He entered his old room, the posters of his favourite rock artist still on the wall, his football jersey from "the game" he had won for the team in his college days. His trophies, marking all his triumphs during his schooling years, some from the start of his career, and a degree of law on his wall, a career he never pursued, for his love of detective work.

The whole night, Charles could not sleep. The video of his father being shot kept playing in his head on a loop, as if a never-ending nightmare of reality, the pain of which would never be forgotten.

There is something amiss, it's not right. He did not make a run for it or try to save himself. What did the other person say that made him feel so helpless? He just accepted his fate. Could he have known this was coming? The thoughts kept repeating in his head. He lay on his bed, staring at the ceiling, and finally dozed off.

The next morning, Charles went to the bathroom to get ready for the day's routine. He had a splitting headache, but the thoughts of last night and the unanswered questions continued to trouble him. As he walked down to get some coffee, he passed by his father's study and paused, staring at it for a moment. He then entered the kitchen, where Darcy was already present, and Andy was serving her breakfast.

"Rough night. No sleep," Charles said as he walked slowly across the kitchen to get his coffee. He leaned against the kitchen counter with the cup in hand. "I didn't sleep a wink myself. Just miss him so much."

"It just does not make sense to me. Why did he not make a run for it?" Charles mused.

"Maybe he was not able to," Darcy suggested. "The man was shot. He was almost eighty. He must have felt pain and weakness, maybe that's why."

Charles nodded in acknowledgement but remained quiet. He then turned to Andy and asked, "Can you tell me the events of the day, Andy? Try to remember and go through it. Maybe you are missing something."

Andy looked at Darcy in amazement, surprised by the question directed at him. "Well, Master Charles, I was in the adjacent room. He had two meetings that day, apparently. He would always talk loudly with everyone. That was his tone. All I heard was him talking with someone in the first meeting, and then in the second one, again, he was talking loudly. They were at it for some time. Then there was silence, and then I barely heard them talking. I thought the meeting was over, and the next thing I heard scares me still."

"How much time was the person in there?" Charles inquired.

"The first one was about 15 minutes long. Then a gap, then the second one again for about the same time," Andy explained.

"He did not ask you to bring anything—tea, water, or coffee—while he was with them?" Charles probed further.

"He rings the bell when he needs anything. It seems a bit out of place, but he did not ring for anything during the second meeting," Andy replied.

"Did you hear anything at all? What was the argument about, and with whom?" Charles asked.

"The walls are quite thick, especially in his study," Andy responded.

"What do you mean, thick?"

"You know how Master Robert was. He asked them to be made, as you children say, thicker, and he made them soundproof for his clients. That is why I heard a low bang and not the full sound of a gunshot. He didn't want anyone to hear what he was advising them. He would never allow me to come into the room while the meetings were going on. The meeting would always start after I finished my service. Till then, the pleasantries would be exchanged. I would only go in again when the master rang for the service. To him, privacy was everything. You know how he loved to be secretive about everything he did or wanted to do."

Charles nodded in agreement. "He and all his secrets, his mysteries, his games, his treasure hunts with us when we were kids. He was a brilliant man, no doubt, but now his death itself is a mystery."

"Since Master Robert was dealing with all types of clients, good and bad, he had also increased the security of that room. He made another entrance to the room directly so the client would not wander about in the house. They would come straight in at the time given for the meeting and straight out. *I am paid to represent*, he would always say, *a client is a client. Good or bad is for the court to decide, not me.*"

"Did you see who was in the room with him in the meeting?"

"No, that meeting was a short one of sorts. It may have been with his partner, Cliff. I am not sure, but I saw his car parked outside, and like I said, the walls are quite thick. You can only hear muffled voices."

"How about before that?"

"Yes, I did, when I served tea. I gave his description to the deputies as well."

"He was a fairly old person in his late fifties, maybe, with curly white hair, slim built, had both his ears pierced, and seemed to speak with a bit of a southern accent. He had a tattoo on his right ring finger."

"That matches the description of Don Arthur," said Darcy.

"Paulo, you mean Don Arthur Paulo? He is on bail for a dozen cases. A history sheeter."

"Yes, he was one of father's clients. Now you know why he is still out. That's how good father was."

"What, him? But why him? Was father in some trouble? What did he get himself into, Darcy?"

"Didn't you hear what Andy just said about him? *A client is a client*," Darcy said, imitating Robert.

"There's another thing you should know: Master Charles and Master Robert also bought a gun in his name. It was clipped under his table. He kept it just in case the need arose to protect himself. I did not share this with the deputies because I was under a lot of stress, and it slipped out of my mind completely."

"Why didn't you tell me this before, Andy?" Charles shouted, "I have to report this and get things in order. You are only making it more and more difficult for yourself, Andy."

"Calm down, Charles. Everyone was confused last night. Give him some benefit of the doubt."

"But the deputies searched every inch of the area in that study. There was no gun found at the crime scene."

"Then, Master Charles, it can be assumed that the killer took it with him."

"Andy, do you have anything—any document to show—about all the changes he has made to his study room? Maybe we can find something worthwhile there."

"I don't think there would be anything particular, but let me go through the papers and see if I can find something. I will look for it, Master Charles, and keep it in your old hiding place."

"And that was years ago. I am not a small boy now. Just keep them on father's desk.

"For me, you always will be, Master Charles." Andy pulled a chair from the dining table. "Please sit down and have your breakfast. You need the energy to go about and handle all this. If you need anything, I will be in my room." Andy served breakfast and left the room.

"What are you thinking, Darcy? You seem a bit lost in your thoughts."

"I just miss him a lot, Charles. Everyone can console us, but no one knows the pain we feel."

"I understand what you are feeling, Darcy. It's just too much."

"Yeah, it does seem like the killer is a very smart person," said Darcy.

"We do have two rather weak leads, one Don Paulo and the other, his partner, Cliff, from the two meetings he had."

The doorbell rang.

"I will get it. Please finish your breakfast," said Andy.

Andy came back and said, "There is a Miss Lisa here to see you, Master Charles."

"Send her in, Andy."

"Lisa, is it? I didn't know you two were a thing already!" said Darcy in a light tone, struggling to smile a bit.

"Oh! There's nothing like that. We are just taking things as they come along. What about your boyfriend, Darcy? What was his name? I forgot."

"Ex-boyfriend, you mean? It is not worth remembering his name."

"When did this happen? You never told me anything!"

"A month ago. I was always too occupied with my business, according to him. The business was going down, and he could not understand that it needed my attention."

"You always were a strong one, no doubt about it, doing whatever it takes!"

"Wish he understood that, Charles. I was only trying for a better life, but he chose to walk away."

Charles rolled his eyes as if indicating, "Good riddance to bad rubbish!"

Lisa walked into the room, hugged and kissed Charles on the cheek. "You look drained."

"You are a sight for sore eyes. That's Darcy, my sister."

"Hi, Darcy, I heard a lot about you! How are you guys holding up?"

"Just hanging by," said Darcy.

Darcy got up and said, "I will be in my room if needed. We have to think about his funeral now, Charles."

"Yeah, let's get it over with, and then I can concentrate on finding who did this."

"Hi, you!" said Lisa while hugging Charles tightly and giving him a little peck on the cheek. "I have missed you. I am here for you no matter what, you know that right?"

Charles nodded and, while gazing deeply into her eyes, leaned in and kissed her lips. "You are my strength right now. Just your presence gives me the assurance that everything will be okay. This too shall pass."

Lisa nodded in agreement while moving her hands through Charles' hair. "I cannot imagine the pain you are in right now, but give it time. The answers will come. Darcy also needs you right now. You have to be strong. You both are now the support for each other."

Charles rested his head on Lisa's shoulder and closed his eyes, trying to get that one minute of calm in all the madness going around.

"There are a lot of questions that I need answers to, Lisa!"

Lisa pulled him up lovingly from her shoulder and whispered politely, "First things first, let's get the funeral over with."

They both got up and climbed the staircase to go into Darcy's room. They opened the door to find Darcy near the wardrobe, pushing some things in.

"Always over-shopping, you will never change," smiled Charles.

"And always pointing it out," retorted Darcy, quickly closing the wardrobe door. "I was looking for my black attire for the funeral. It seems like it's getting used more often now."

All three of them discussed the arrangements for the funeral, how things would be carried out, who would be invited, and how to proceed with it. They divided their duties and got to the task at hand.

"Maybe Andy can help with this. He might have a list of his friends and close acquaintances, like his phonebook," said Charles.

"Yeah! He did carry the little phonebook in his pocket all the time. That could be helpful," replied Darcy.

Darcy picked up the intercom and explained everything to Andy. She asked Andy to look for the phonebook if it was not in evidence with the police and help with the arrangements for the funeral to be held the day after.

Chapter 2

The Funeral

On the day of the funeral, the skies were grey and sorrowful. The weather was mild, with a calming, cool breeze. A good soul had passed.

It was an open casket. His body was all cleaned up and suited. A picture of their deceased mother holding hands with Robert was kept next to the casket. It was a fairly small gathering, all dressed in black, with close relations and sadness all across the courtyard of the mansion. Everyone loved him, he had a gentle soul. He had a limited number of friends, but all of them were special to him. The one common thing binding them all was his helpfulness to them, no matter the situation.

Charles was in his room, sitting on the bed, staring at his gun, wondering if he should keep it or not. After his father's murder, he felt exposed without it. This was the only thing left that he could trust his life on—a partner of sorts.

Feeling anxious and troubled, he got up and put it in the drawer. He realised there were a lot of people downstairs waiting to meet him and Darcy, and a gun had no place in an event of peace and condolences. He then proceeded downstairs for the funeral.

Charles, Darcy, and Lisa sat in the front row, with the entire crowd behind them. A deputy walked up to Charles and said, "These were the belongings of your father. The captain asked me to give it to you personally and tell you nothing was found in the postmortem other than the bullet wound to his chest. That was the cause of his death. There was a small pressure mark in his hand, but it could have been from the closed fist."

"Thanks," said Charles, handing the things to Andy. He turned around and waved to the captain in acknowledgement.

He turned around and said, "That's strange. Everyone from his firm seems to be here, except Cliff. What could be more important than the funeral of his partner? That does raise suspicion."

"One thing at a time, Charles, let's just get this funeral over with. We cannot accuse people just for their absence. We need some reasonable cause."

"Some of his big-shot clients are here too. He did have the best of the good guys and the notorious ones. Really kept a good balance."

The service went smoothly, and everyone paid their respects to the deceased.

Andy walked up to Charles and said, "It's time for the eulogy. Then we can lower the casket. He always wanted to be buried near the outhouse."

Charles nodded in agreement. Charles, Darcy, and Lisa got up and walked to the front to address the crowd. Darcy stepped behind Charles and said, "I can't face them. I am too emotional."

"It's alright!" said Lisa, holding her hand in reassurance.

Charles adjusted the mic on the podium to speak, "Today, I address you all with a very heavy heart. I never thought this day would come so soon, and I never imagined it would be under such circumstances. Here lies a multi-faceted man, a loving father, a loving husband, a caring family man, a helpful friend, and a ferocious lawyer.

Those who knew him knew he was always there when you needed him. He would never turn away a person in need. Family before all, he would always say and never back down from a commitment. Always smiling, always joyful, and always happy, no matter the situation.

As I said, a ferocious lawyer, if he knew the person was innocent no matter the background, good or bad, rich or poor, would give his life to save them, but he was very stubborn in his ways. He always had to do things his traditional way and never change.

He was a loving father who would give as much time as he could for his family. When we were kids, he would give us small puzzles to play with and he would ask me and Darcy to come on small treasure hunts with him, with indications hidden all over the mansion for us to find. That was his way of playing with us, teaching us, and spending time with us, whatever he could spare. He would then reward us with chocolates and toys for our triumphs.

As we grew older, the games intensified and made us work our minds to the limit to find the answers. He would ask us to look for answers where we thought there were none and had overlooked them. *Relax your mind, empty it, and think. Empty space has all the answers*, he would always emphasise and keep pushing us until we found what we were looking for. *Work as a team,* he would always scold me and Darcy if we fought.

As we grew older, we grew apart, but never far. He would write handwritten letters to Darcy and me. We would make fun of them when we met him, and we would ask him to email us or maybe just call.

In today's day and age, who writes letters? We would ask him this. Why not learn a little bit about modern ways? They won't hurt, but he would strongly condemn the idea. He would never agree, the strong-headed man he was, always in love with his pen, paper, and his big, fat books. He always despised modern ways, saying they took away the charm of things. He always replied, *Remember the old ways too while you learn the new ones. Don't forget them because something easier just came along.*

The letters he sent us had very strong attachments to them. For us, they were always a piece of paper and some ink scribbled. More often than not, they would contain some, as he would call them, practice directions, for us to follow in life.

That was his way of showing us he cared and remembered. *They are treasures*, he would always retort, *you will understand their value the day I am gone.*

Today, that day has come, and yes, I understand what you meant now. Today, we miss everything about you, father... just one more day, one more hour, and one more letter. Your loud laughter, your insistent know-it-all nature...

When you sneezed, father, the mansion shook as if to gather itself from what had happened."

The small gathering smiled, tears streaming down their cheeks.

Just then, as the speech was going on, a little movement was seen in the bushes behind the crowd.

"Bang"... A gun was fired at a distance, and before anyone could even move or react to the sound of the fire, a bullet flew swiftly past Charles.

"Get down!" shouted Charles. Everyone, on the contrary, got up and started to run around in panic. Charles looked around to look for the shooter.

"Charles! She has been shot!" shouted Darcy while holding Lisa on the floor. Charles turned around to see Lisa down on the floor with her arm covered in blood. For a moment, Charles could not believe his eyes. The sound of voices around him blurred in the background.

"Charles! Charles!" shouted Darcy. Charles finally came to his senses, fright on his face, sweat going down his cheek. He slowly moved towards Lisa.

"No! Lisa! No, not her!" He checked her vitals. They seemed fine. He checked her wound. Her arm was grazed by the bullet, and the cut was deep. Charles quickly removed his tie and tied it tightly around Lisa's arm above the wound. Lisa grunted a bit.

"Darcy, please keep pressure on it."

Darcy put her hand on the wound and pressed it down.

"Lisa passed out because of the shock. She is bleeding, but it is a flesh wound. Stay with her, I'll call for help. Stay low. You are safe behind the wall here. I need to find out who did this."

"Don't worry at all. You go look. I am here with her and look, Andy is also coming. We will be fine."

Charles waved at Andy to come and stay with the girls.

Charles ran behind the sitting area to see if there was anyone there. He spotted something moving in the bushes and ran towards them. He heard a sound behind him and turned. Just then, a man jumped out from behind the bushes and hit Charles on the head. He was knocked down on the ground. A few seconds later, Charles came to his senses, his vision blurry, and saw a person running. Charles slowly came back to his feet and tried to run after him.

"Get him! Stop him!" he shouted as he followed him, but with all the panic and everyone running, no one could hear Charles or even distinguish him from the crowd. Charles quickly patted the side of his waist for his gun and then cursed himself that he left it in his room.

"Damn! Why did I leave it? I could have gotten it. When will I stop making such mistakes?" Charles tried his best but he lost the man in the crowd.

Charles went back to where Andy and Darcy were sitting, while a team of medical personnel was examining Lisa.

"Did you get him?"

"No, he got away, Darcy. Maybe the camera got something."

"Did you see his face, at least?"

"No, I could not. He ambushed me from behind!"

"Oh God! Are you okay? You can't put your life in danger like this, Charles."

Lisa started moving a bit, and Charles moved closer to her.

"Hey!" she said softly.

"Don't move, just relax. You are okay and safe now," said Charles.

"What happened?"

"You were shot. The bullet grazed your arm. It's a little deep, and you passed out due to shock."

"Shot!!! What?" said Lisa in panic. "How?"

"There was a shooter here, but he missed. There must be an angel watching over us. I'm sorry to drag you into all this, Lisa. I didn't know this would happen."

Lisa pulled herself up, holding Charles. “It’s not your fault. No one could have predicted this. It’s a funeral. Someone has to be a very rotten breed to attack a funeral.”

“She is going to be fine, it’s only a flesh wound. But we would like to keep her under observation for some time. She needs rest too!” said the nurse, treating and checking on Lisa.

“Sure. Andy will help you take her to the room for now. It’s not safe outside for her. The killer might still be around.” They both lifted Lisa up and took her carefully to the room inside the mansion.

“What the hell is happening, Charles? What did father get himself into? What was he dealing with?”

“I don’t know, Darcy,” Charles replied, frightened. “Things are really spiralling down. That man was here to kill us, and I need to find out why. Why would he attack Lisa? Nothing makes sense at the moment.”

“Relax, Charles. The reinforcements are here now. We are safe. Gather yourself and think calmly.”

“All the answers are here. That is why the killer came back. We just need to understand what to look for and where to find them.”

“This is just great. Even after his death, our father leaves us with a mystery to solve. I hope it doesn’t kill us first.”

“That’s not the case, Darcy. But we need to move quickly now. Two attacks in a matter of days and no suspects. Someone is watching our every move and wants us dead. I lost the one person I loved the most. The other two were at risk today. It can't go on like this. I will ask the captain for more security for both of you and maybe even a safe house. I need to keep you both safe."

"No, absolutely not, Charles. I am not going anywhere and leaving you alone, exposed like this. We are fine and capable of looking after ourselves. There are no safe houses. You concentrate on the killer. Let's just finish the funeral. Let father at least rest peacefully."

Charles got up and shook the dust off him. He asked whoever was left to gather around. Charles signalled to lower the casket to the ground and cover it up. He and Darcy put a fistful of mud on it first, while the others followed suit. The casket was then covered up fully. Darcy then put a wreath on the grave, and they all went inside the mansion.

Charles went into the living room and called the captain. The captain was already aware of what happened, even though he left early. He was equally shocked and puzzled. Charles asked the captain for security at the mansion to protect Lisa and Darcy since they refused to shift to a safe house, to which the captain happily agreed.

"Don't you worry, Charles. You have the help of the entire police force now. We are all up and vigilant, given the spree of attacks on your family. I will have two patrol cars posted outside the mansion at all times. Things are getting out of hand, and we cannot accept it lying down. You take care of the case. I will personally see to it that everyone else remains safe."

"Thanks, Captain," Charles said, hanging up the phone.

Charles then called up the deputy in the evidence department.

"Do you have all the reports now and the surveillance? I need them ASAP. Do you understand? ... Yes, that's good. Bring me what you have at the earliest. I need to get started on this mystery before anyone else is attacked."

Charles then put his head back on the high chair and, with his eyes closed, tried to fall asleep. But the events of the day keep playing in his head again and again. The restlessness just didn't go away. The guilt of not being able to capture the culprit and putting his family in danger really troubled him.

Charles decided to go up to his room, where Lisa was resting. When he entered, Lisa turned to him.

"Hey, Lisa, how are you feeling?"

"I'm better. Just a lot of pain in the arm and lots of painkillers in my body," she said with a soft smile.

"Rest as much as you can and get better. You are safe here now. I cannot tell you how sorry I am—sorry that I could not protect you!" Charles started to cry, his eyes were all teary and red.

Lisa hugged him. "No one could have foreseen this. You need rest too, Charles. How will you capture the culprit if you are not in the right state of mind? Rest a bit."

"I am trying, Lisa, but I just can't get my head around everything that has happened. It's scary how close death is at all times. You took it so bravely and are still here. Anyone else would have been miles away by now."

"We are safe now, Charles. Just relax for the night and start fresh tomorrow. There is security outside now. The doors and windows are shut. The room is safe."

Charles agreed with Lisa's comforting words and lay down in bed with her. He hugged Lisa. She held his hand and kissed him. "Rest now, please."

Charles kissed her on the neck and turned off the lights. They both cuddled and tried to sleep.

Chapter 3

The Evidence and the Vague Truth

The next day, Captain Nate, along with a deputy, came to meet Charles with all the evidence they gathered in the house on the day of the crime. Charles and the deputy sat at the table in the common room, looking at all the evidence piece by piece.

"How are you holding up, Charles? How are Lisa and Darcy?"

"Hanging by a thread, Captain. Things just keep going from bad to worse, and I have nothing—nothing to show, nothing to investigate, no leads, nothing. Darcy and Lisa...

Oh God, they have been just so strong and have supported me unconditionally through it all. Lisa is recovering well, and Darcy is all over the place like a fanatic, trying to find answers and helping me in any way possible. I don't blame her, we all want this solved as soon as possible."

"Well, we bring some hope. Sorry, Charles, but it's very little to start with."

"Let us start somewhere, at least, Captain. Maybe if we put our heads together, we can figure something out."

They took out the files and folders from the bag to show them to Charles.

"So what about the cufflink we found under the table? Did you lift the prints of that?" asked Charles.

"Well, that's the weirdest thing. It had nothing on it. It came clean with no prints."

"But how can that be? It has to have something on it—some prints, a bit of blood, some residue, or fibre."

"Nope, not even a smidge of anything at all," replied the captain.

"How is that even possible? That was the main piece of evidence and the best chance to catch the killer. You saw that my father had ripped off the killer's shirt. It had to have traces of something on it."

"That baffles me too, Charles. It's almost as if it were wiped clean of everything."

"But then what about the torn shirt, Captain? If my father pulled the cufflink, where is the piece of that shirt? Did you find any fabric in the room?"

"Yes, while sweeping for evidence, the forensics found a few threads of white fabric on the sleeve of the suit your father was wearing that night, but we could not find any piece of the fabric on the floor, in the room, or nearby. Until we find the shirt or anything related to it, we can't even connect the threads to the shirt of the shooter."

"So you mean we have squat, nothing, zilch, zero? Do you realise this is my father? God!" Charles banged his fists on the table. "And you found nothing for me to go on about?"

"What happened?" Darcy came running in a panic to the room. "I heard a sound."

"Charles!" said Captain Nate in a stern tone. "We are trying our best to do what we can. You know you have the full department backing you on this. Even with the slightest evidence or lead, rest assured, we will investigate it. But be very clear: you have to keep your anger and emotions in check before the superior officer. I told you this from the beginning."

Charles turned to Darcy and said, "It's the cufflink, the only piece of evidence, and it doesn't even have a speck of anything on it. It's as if the evidence vanished into thin air."

"This just keeps getting weirder and weirder. I am really concerned," said Darcy.

"I still don't understand it, Captain. How can the cufflink be completely clean? Maybe there is someone in the department working with the killer."

"No, Charles," Captain Nate said angrily. "This is going too far. How can you even suggest that when you yourself bagged the cufflink for the forensics? We are all with you. How many times do I have to repeat that to you? I understand the emotional trauma you are going through, but pointing a finger at my department, that's not acceptable."

"I apologise, Captain. You are right. It's just that my whole family is depending on me to solve this, and I don't want to let them down. I have to find my father's killer at any cost."

"You are trying your best, Charles," said Darcy.

"One more thing, did the report come back on the composition of the cufflink?"

The deputy opened a file and pointed to a line. "It's silver. Why do you ask?"

"Because my father had them made for, god knows who all, and this just narrows down the suspect list to some twenty to thirty people at least. He gave them to his workers, his friends, and his colleagues, even to me and Darcy and his partner, Cliff Dreker, basically anyone he ever liked."

"At least it is a start, and we start questioning all of them. Maybe we can get a few leads," said the captain.

"What about the bullet casing found at the crime scene?"

"Well, Charles, that does match the gun registered to your father. The one stated by Andy. It is a magnum, but we still haven't found the gun. We have swept the area inside out—the sewage, the gardens, the bins, everything nearby—but still haven't found the damn thing."

"I understand, Captain. So, no prints and no murder weapon. It's not even a little bit. I have nothing to start with."

"It was your father's gun. Maybe someone else had access to it? What about Andy? He reported knowing about it later, if you remember."

"Are you suggesting Andy had something to do with this? Andy is here. If he were guilty, he would have already left or run away, but he did not, and he is fully cooperating with the investigation. Plus, it was under his table, clipped, and not inside a safe. Anyone could have taken it if they knew about it. If only we had eyes inside the room, we would have known what exactly happened."

"But Andy was the only one in the adjacent room to your father. That does put him under strong suspicion, and in normal circumstances, he would have been detained."

"If he is the killer, then he is here. But I would request that you only arrest him once you have irrefutable proof of his guilt. He is literally in house arrest with the patrol cars outside."

"Agreed," nodded the captain.

"What about the footage from the cameras on the day my father was shot?"

"Well, two people came to see him that day, Don Paulo and Cliff, his partner. Paulo left after a meeting of about eighteen minutes and forty-five seconds (shows him the footage of him arriving and leaving). He was perfectly fine after that. Even Andy must have seen him when he went in after the meeting to pick up the cups. He was one of your father's clients, and it's not a far stretch of an imagination that he did this. Unfortunately, he is overseas now and out of our jurisdiction currently. Well, you know we are still looking through the footage again and again, but there is something I wish to show you. Remember when Robert was shot? He was seen arguing with someone. Well, moments before, we saw his partner Cliff enter the house."

"Why did you not start with that, Captain? That gives us a prime suspect."

"Hold your horses, Charles. He is also seen almost at the door, see (pauses the footage and zooms). Seconds after the shot was fired. See there. He comes in his car, gets out, and goes inside the mansion (fast forwards). See there, he comes back, and by the way of his walk and demeanour, it shows that he was in no hurry and was completely calm. Even after an argument, if he had anything to do with the shooting or if he heard it, he would have panicked, run to his car, or raised an alarm, but nothing. He just seems to be walking casually to his car with his phone in hand. But on the flip side, being the good lawyer that he is, he understands the mind of a criminal. Maybe he knew if he ran out in panic, the police would have definitely arrested him. This diffuses the tension and suspicion."

"Both versions are equally possible, Captain."

"The camera shows Cliff leaving after seventeen minutes and ten seconds. Andy said the meeting went on for about fifteen minutes. So, that's about right, give or take a few minutes. That much error can be factored in."

"Yeah. Did you try to call Cliff or reach him at least?"

"You think we didn't try? He is a lawyer, just like your father. He has been successfully dodging us ever since the murder. He is not home. He is not answering his phone, and we are looking for him."

"That is really suspicious. Captain, do you think he is hiding something?"

"It could be... but we have nothing that makes him look guilty at the moment, just suspicious. He was at the mansion when your father was shot, and we have that footage with us. Maybe he realised that."

"But it gives you a probable cause at least?"

"Why do you think we are calling and trying to get in touch with him, Charles?" said the captain sarcastically.

"There is more, Charles. On the day of the funeral, when Lisa was shot, the garden camera caught a person wearing a black jacket jumping over the fence."

"Show it to him," the captain gestured to the deputy. (She shows the footage to Charles.)

"See, but it's at a distance because there is only one camera there, so it's blurry. See there: you are standing, giving your speech. There's gunfire. There's Lisa falling and Darcy is grabbing her. Now look here while you are running. He jumps from behind that bush, see, and hits you on the head and then over the fence. See there."

"Yeah, he was the guy. Maybe he was the one who shot my father too, but why come back the next day? I keep thinking about this again and again. Maybe he left some piece of evidence at the mansion."

"It could be one of the reasons, Charles. But then why shoot anyone? Why not just quietly sneak in and take the evidence and leave? Have you considered the possibility that the killer was trying to scare you to back off? I cannot comprehend why he would shoot Lisa. She is not part of the family yet. Then why her? Your life could be in danger, Charles."

"You mean the acts of father, to be compensated by the son."

"Now the interesting part: the bullet was recovered from the wall behind the podium. It was a Magnum bullet, but we could not find the casing in the bushes. Maybe the killer took it with him."

"So that's it. He has my father's gun. That's why we have not found it yet. And the camera footage from outside the room showed him wearing a black suit with a white shirt, it has to be him. Finally, a lead."

"At this point, anything is possible, Charles. We cannot rule out anything, but we do have a motive now. Someone wanted Robert dead, and they are after his family too now. Are you sure you have no idea what was happening? One attempt and one successful kill. Same gun."

"No, Cap, it baffles me too. How could father get into all this with such kinds of people? He was never the bad type. I really don't know what got into him."

"What about the FA initials on the computer? Does anyone match the description yet?"

"No, no leads are there till now. But maybe when we start talking to the people with the cufflinks, we can find out something more."

"I'll just say this point blank to you, Charles. I think you should go to a safe house with Lisa and Darcy and leave the investigation to us."

"Captain, I can't stop investigating. It's my father. I don't care, even if they kill me. If you want, you can move Darcy and Lisa to the safe house, that is, again, if they agree to go. We feel safe here. We have security outside. No one comes or leaves without checking. In a way, this has become a safe house. Plus, if there is anything to be found, it has to be here in this mansion. If I leave and the killer comes back, I will never find him again. Maybe that is why he came back. There has to be something here."

"You may be right, Charles."

The captain sighed and got up. Charles got up too.

"I knew you would not agree. You are too stubborn to give up anyway. Just be careful, keep an eye over your shoulder, and don't travel alone. The patrol cars are outside. Take their help, they don't bite."

"Yeah, yeah, I know. Trust you guys. Thanks, Captain, for everything. Much appreciated. You try to question the leads and look for this black jacket guy. Maybe he has the gun and used it to kill my father. Leave Cliff to me. I'll find him and make him talk, and if I find something, I will call you. Till then, put a trace on his phone, will you?"

"You do that," said the captain. "I will get a warrant for the trace."

The captain and the deputy left the mansion.

"It has to be that bastard Cliff. He did something, and it cost our father his life. That is why the killer keeps coming back because Cliff has also ghosted everyone."

"We can't point fingers like this, Darcy. Although he and the shooter have some connection, I will find out. I will try to get in touch with him, but we have to be careful now. The shooter is on the hunt and maybe after us."

"You do that, Charles. I have a few errands to run. I will see you later in the evening, and before you start lecturing me, I will be careful and will take one of the patrol cars with me, I promise."

Charles smiles. "Can't it wait? I want you to stay safe and inside only. Have Andy do it."

"Nah, it's a bank thing. I have to sign and all. And since you are too busy to ask, brother, Lisa is better off having breakfast with Andy in the dining room. Be with her, Charles. She needs you, too. This is too much for her. Take care of her, please."

"Oh God!!! Lisa, I forgot about her completely with all this evidence discussion. I will do that," nodded Charles in agreement.

"Charles, would it be okay if we had a small barbeque tonight, just us three? We can relax a bit and just have a quiet dinner. I'll prepare everything. It will give us a chance to be at peace."

Charles nodded in agreement, and Darcy left, giving him a side hug.

Charles goes to the dining room to eat with Lisa.

"Hi, love, how are you feeling?"

"I'm good, getting stronger by the day and fatter by the hour since Andy refuses to serve bad-tasting food and I gobble down everything."

Charles smiled and said, "You need it. I cannot apologise enough for what I have put you through."

"Well, they say you should find out what you are marrying into. Now I know I have to get a prenup with you, with the only condition of not getting me killed."

They both started giggling, and Andy smiled seeing them like that.

Charles turned to Andy and said, "You take good care of her. I will be back soon."

"Will do, Master Charles."

"Andy, I hope you are not hiding any more facts from me."

"I swear, I am not, Master Charles, and I never will. I was scared that night, but I am in my senses fully now."

"Did you find anything else in our father's papers?"

"Not yet. I am looking for it every day, with just millions of papers to go through. Master Robert never threw anything."

"Let me know if you find anything."

Charles leaned in and kissed Lisa on the lips. "Get better soon, love, and then maybe we can go for a nice quiet vacation once all of this is over."

"That would be splendid. We need a break. Let's do that soon. Maybe Darcy will also agree to come along."

Charles nodded in agreement and headed out. Before he went, Darcy invited them to a barbeque on the terrace.

"I know, it would be good to calm our nerves a bit. Things have been rough."

Charles left the mansion to look for Cliff.

Chapter 4

The Cliffhanger

Charles got into his car to go to his father's office. While driving, he tried to call Cliff, but he did not answer. He tried again, but the phone kept going to voicemail. He sent Cliff a text to call back urgently, which was delivered and read, but no response came from him.

Charles then called his secretary at the office, but again, no one picked up the phone. He then called his father's secretary, who picked up the phone, "Mr Knight's office."

"Hi, this is Charles, Robert's son. I wish to come and ask about a few things. Is that alright?"

"Hi, Charles, it's Norma. You are most welcome, child. Please come."

"Why isn't Cliff answering his phone?"

"Come here, and we will talk."

"I am on my way. Be there in another fifteen minutes."

Charles reached the building and entered the lobby. He then took the lift to the 10th floor. On getting out, his eyes got moist seeing his father's name and a big portrait of him on the wall. Charles stayed still for a few seconds, gazing at his father's portrait.

"No frame could hold him, I always said. Such a grand persona," smiled Norma. "Hi Charles, you are all grown up now, aren't you? I still remember when Robert made you run around the office for a piece of candy."

Charles hugged Norma.

"I wish we could have met under better circumstances."

Norma was Robert's secretary from the first year he joined practice. He saved her from a murder conviction that was falsely pinned on her. Since then, she has been with him, helping people in need and being falsely accused.

"It's been ages since I have seen you. You haven't aged a bit."

"Like father, like son, flattery," smiled Norma.

They both laugh gently and walk down to the conference room. They took a seat, and Norma asked Charles what he would like to have.

"Maybe a drink of my father's favourite?"

Norma poured him a glass of scotch for Charles and sat next to him.

"It's sad how the tables have turned for the worst. This place was so happy, always buzzing and always lively, clients coming in, bills being raised, everyone was just so happy, and Robert, oh God, Robert," Norma started to weep. "He was the lifeline of everyone. He always kept everyone uplifted, old or young. Everyone just loved him. 'Represent the client' (Charles also repeats with Norma), that's all you are paid to do."

Charles nodded, "Yeah, that was his big one. He repeated it again and again, with all the confidence in the world."

"Who would do such a thing, Charles? He was a loving man. Sure, he had some bad clients, but as all criminal lawyers do, that's where the money is. He never asked a poor man to leave either. He would happily pay from his own pockets."

"I am trying my best to find out, trust me. But I am desperate now. We have no leads, and all that we have is non-conclusive evidence to point at anyone. Tell me about Cliff, Norma. I have not been able to get in touch with him. The police are looking for him. He is not answering his calls, nor is he responding. He is one of the prime suspects now since he was at the mansion on the day of the incident."

"Cliff? Why him?"

"He was seen leaving father's study when he was shot."

"Cliff does come across as someone who you may suspect of foul play because of his aggressive nature, but trust me, he has a good heart. Your father trusted him with the affairs of the firm and discussed everything with him. The day it happened, he left here in the evening at the usual time and must have met Robert at the mansion. He did seem in a bit of a hurry and tensed, maybe it was a case or something. I was not privy to their conversations."

"I know. I know, my father and his privacy issues."

Agreeing with Charles, Norma continued, "So Cliff left, and since that day, he has not come. He has had some financial troubles lately, but there is nothing that he cannot handle himself. I mean, that would not motivate him to do something like this."

"What about his secretary? Maybe she knows something?"

"His secretary came the next day and quit her job."

"That is suspicious."

"No, she had just joined a month ago. Cliff keeps his secretaries really busy, and they just burn out over the year. He goes through them like crazy. He can't help it. Everyone has a lot of work. If you wish to speak to her, you can wait. She is coming in an hour to pick up her stuff. As for Cliff, I can't say where he is. Maybe she has an idea."

"Alright, I'll wait for her. Norma, if you see or notice anything unusual, please let me know. It will be of great help."

"Will do. Why don't you wait in your father's office? I will let you know when she comes."

Charles nodded and walked to his father's office. He opened the door and just got lost in all the fun and happy memories of the past. The way Robert used to play and make him hunt for small treasures, indications, and games. "Next one, Charles, next one, think, think," said Robert in a faded recollection.

Charles did not realise the time, sitting on his father's chair, going through the fond memories.

"Charles, Charles, she is here," said Norma, bringing him back to the present.

"Bring her in, please."

"Hi, please have a seat."

"I do not wish to say anything without my lawyer. You guys have eaten my head enough. One month, and this is the torture I have to bear."

"I haven't even asked you anything," said Charles. "Sit down, have a drink, and relax. We will talk later. We are all family here. No police work."

"It's alright," said Norma, while handing her a drink. "You can trust him. He is here as a son and not as a detective."

"I already told you guys what I knew. Everything was normal. Cliff left after his day of usual work and did not return the next day. I came in two days after that but could not reach him, and the police were after my life as if I had asked him to run off. This is why I left. I can't bear all this and so much of it. He was a good man, but I had nothing to do with it."

"We know. Please relax. All I want to know is if you have the slightest idea where Cliff could be."

"No, I don't. He did not tell me. I told you he left just like any other day—nothing new. Always in a hurry, always."

"Okay. Let me put it this way: could there be any place he could have gone or could be hiding? A friend, a relative, or anyone else he ever mentioned?"

"Not that I know of. His private life was his own. He never shared any details. Although... (she looked at Norma), he did have me pay an electricity bill for a lodge up in the woods. It was in his mother's name. He had asked me to pay for it."

"Awesome, that's something. Thank you. Do you have a copy of the bill?"

"Yes, I'll get it for you. It's in his office in the bills files."

The secretary walked out of the room to get the bill.

"I told you she was clean, Charles. We have been seasoned in this office. A newbie can never take this kind of pressure, plus the additional factor of the police questioning her. She rightfully succumbed to it."

"Yeah, you are right. It's not easy for her at all."

The secretary came back with a paper in hand and said, "There you go. Can I leave now and be at peace?"

"Yes, thank you for all your help. I will ask the detectives to trouble you only if needed," Charles smiled and thanked her and Norma.

"Norma, why are you still here? I know you are not being paid."

"Well, someone has to look after his things till all of this is over. Consider it a payback for all that he has done for me."

Charles got up and hugged Norma before leaving. "Take care. I will see you soon. Do come by the mansion when you get time. We can have a nice dinner."

Just as Charles was about to walk out, his phone rang. It was the captain. "Charles, we have a hit on Cliff's phone. He is somewhere in the woods."

"It's his mother's lodge, Captain."

"Yes, but how did you know? Are you hiding something again, Charles?"

"No, I just found out from his papers in the office that he has a lodge there. I was just about to call you only."

"Okay, see you there then."

Charles got in his car and drove up the mountain road. The captain, along with his deputy, caught up with Charles and signalled him to follow them. They reached the lodge, but it was a big estate with a huge gate. There was a driveway that led to the lodge on the far side of the estate.

"This isn't what I was expecting," the captain remarked as he got out of his car to ring the bell, but no one answered.

"We will need a warrant to go in, Charles. You know the drill," the captain said.

"We can't wait, Captain. We know he is hiding there. He will run away. He already knows we are here—you rang the bell yourself," Charles responded.

"If you get caught, Charles, know this: I was never here," the captain said.

"Agreed."

The captain gave Charles a boost, and he climbed up the gate and jumped inside. The captain and the deputy moved back and hid. Charles carefully walked inside, anticipating an ambush, and entered the room from the side window. No one seemed to be there. He saw the gate button and opened it so that the captain could come in.

He searched the lodge again until the captain came in, but found no one. "It's empty, Captain. There is no one here."

"What! The signal is coming from inside and still is. Maybe he is hiding. Let's look for him," the captain suggested.

They searched around the house in different directions. Charles then called the captain. "Hey, Cap, the signal is coming from here because his phone is here, and the food on the table seems fresh. He heard us and left. Maybe check out the back."

"I'll check the back. He would not have gotten far," said the captain, storming out. He signalled for his deputy to go around the back.

Charles picked up the phone, and it was unlocked.

The captain came back. "Nothing, he is gone. His car is still here. He could not have gone far on foot. I have asked the deputy to call for backup and set up a perimeter."

"The phone is formatted, it's clean."

"Give it to me. Let me send it to the tech team. Maybe they can recover something."

Charles handed over the phone to the captain. "God, this is so frustrating... Aaaahhhh."

"We will find him," the captain reassured him. He picked up the police radio and said, "I need to look out for Cliff Dreker. I am sending you his picture now. He should not leave the city at any cost."

"Copy that," said the operator on the police radio.

The captain and Charles did a quick sweep of the lodge again, just in case they missed something, and came back outside.

"Charles, we will find him. I understand your frustration. He is not going anywhere. It's just a matter of time before we nab him," the captain said.

Charles did not respond. He just sat in his car and drove off, irritated and angry. While driving down the dark road, he saw in his rearview mirror that someone has been following his car since he left the lodge.

He saw a small gas station and a coffee shop a few metres ahead. He took the car to the coffee shop for a cup of hot brew. He behaved normally and walked to the shop in a regular manner so as to not alert the person following him. "What the hell is with serial killers and following their target? I am not letting him get away this time," thought Charles.

He realised it could be his father's killer back to kill him, so he had to be very careful and vigilant since he could be armed. He had to be absolutely sure before retaliating. There cannot be any margin of error, or civilians could get hurt.

He walked into the coffee shop and ordered a coffee, then walked back to his car to drive off. The killer did not make his move, but the car still tailed him at a distance. Charles took a quick turn around the corner, stopped his car, immediately got off, and hid before the killer saw him.

A person with a hooded jacket got out of his car, looking around for Charles. Charles was not able to see his face from where he was hiding. Just as the person turned to go away, Charles leaped from behind and pulled his gun to his head. "Hands in the air and do not move an inch. I finally have you. This time, I win."

"It's me, Charles. Don't shoot. It's me, Uncle Cliff. Don't shoot me, please. I just want to talk," he said, removing his hood.

"Uncle Cliff," said Charles in a calm voice. "Why did you not answer my calls? I have tried to contact you several times. Are you okay? Do you know anything about the murder?"

"I will tell you everything I know, but not here," said Cliff. "Let's go somewhere safe where we are not exposed. I understand there is a killer loose."

Charles and Cliff drove back to the lodge. Charles drove ahead, checking for police patrols, but none were spotted. They went inside, closed the doors and blinds, and sat down.

With a serious expression, Charles asked, "Did you kill him?"

Cliff responded aggressively, "Wow, straight to the point, huh?" Then a straight reply, "No, I did not." His response and reaction showed the demeanour of a trained lawyer.

Charles pressed on, "Then why run around and hide like a criminal, Uncle? The police are looking for you everywhere."

Cliff explained, "Are you not seeing what is happening, Charles? Robert was shot dead point-blank, and you all were lucky to have escaped the second attempt. If you were in my shoes and you met Robert moments before he was shot, do you think you would have acted any differently? That captain of yours is no less. He always had a grudge against your father and me for saving so many criminals. He would have arrested me at the drop of a hat and pinned everything on me. He is after blood, as they say. He must be thinking right now that I have the most to gain from all this. He does not realise your father was the soul of the firm. It's dead without him, even if I am there. I can't run the damn thing alone. It will never be the same."

Charles remained sceptical, saying, "Still, Uncle, it doesn't seem right the way you were behaving, hiding from everyone. You made them think you did it."

"When you came to the lodge earlier, I saw you come over the gate. I wanted to talk to you and came out to do so. Then I saw that your captain was also accompanying you. I got scared and ran away. I knew I had to talk to you before the police found me and took me in for questioning. Given the dire circumstances, you are the only one I trust, to be fair."

"It just raises suspicion, Uncle Cliff. You know how the police think. You even missed the funeral. That made things worse."

"Glad I missed it, or it would have been me next to Robert," said Cliff in a shaky voice. "I did not kill him, Charles. I would never... he was my brother, my mentor, a father figure. We always played it hot and cold. He would always be the cool head, and I was the hot one, but that was a facade. I would never touch a hair on him. I loved him like family. I don't have a father. Robert was like a father figure to me. He gave me everything I have today."

Charles, beginning to believe Cliff's innocence, said, "Okay, I trust what you are saying, but you have to understand. I need to be absolutely clear about your innocence. There wasn't much time difference between the shooting and you walking out. What happened that day, Uncle Cliff? Can you tell me in detail, please?"

Cliff hesitated but then spoke, "Yes, but you have to promise me that, assuming the worst against myself, they won't arrest me without cogent proof."

"They won't, Uncle Cliff. You know your rights, and I will make sure of it. Now, what happened? Please, details."

"Well, I went to see your father after work that day. It was a normal meeting and discussion of cases, but with a word of caution for Robert to be careful with the clients he was dealing with recently. He may have thought that if he met them at the mansion, I wouldn't worry about it or find out."

"Don Paulo, you mean?"

"Yes!" exclaimed Cliff. "How did you know about him?"

"Someone in the house recognised him," Charles replied without disclosing Andy's involvement, as he wasn't sure if Cliff could be trusted.

"Anyway, I was there to caution him and convince him to drop Paulo as a client. Paulo is a cunning man, one you do not cross, not even in your dreams."

"But why was my father defending him?"

"I don't know. He never told me. That's why I was there. In all these years working with him, this is the only time he has kept all his meetings with him a secret. He would not meet him in the office, but rather always at the mansion alone. I confronted him that day because I knew it had something to do with Paulo's dirty money, and I could not keep quiet anymore. I told him to get out of all this crap as soon as possible. I was concerned for him and his life. He has represented many clients and made huge sums for us and the firm. We are all indebted to him for everything. I just wanted him to stop dealing with Paulo. He was not the type to be dealt with without caution or an underlying catch. I got a bit aggressive, call it an occupational hazard. He retorted with an equally angry tone, waving his arms around."

Charles remembered the footage, where Robert was seen arguing with someone, moving his arms around, gesturing, and emphasising something.

Even after convincing him so much, he still insisted that he was handling things and everything was in order.

I kept telling and kept insisting, 'You have millions of good clients. They are happy with you and trust you blindly, so why Paulo? It's not as if we need him.'

'You don't need to worry at all, Cliff. I have it all under control,' he said, walking back to his table. I left the study dejected and went to the bathroom."

"How long were you in there?"

"About five or seven minutes. I didn't pay much attention to the time."

Charles understood the reason for Cliff's delay in coming out after leaving the study and why he was only at the gate when the shot was fired. Had he not gone to the bathroom, he would have been long gone before anything happened. But why didn't he run or go back when the shot was fired? He would have heard it. Charles decided to ask him about it to test him and get his version of the story.

"What is still puzzling me, Uncle Cliff, is that you were walking out at the exact moment he was shot. Why didn't you run or go back to him? You walked out calmly, sat in your car, and left."

"Like I told you, I went to the bathroom after the meeting and was there for about five minutes. Then I got a call from the office about some clients wanting urgent relief in a case. He is one of those demanding and high-paying clients. I had my earbuds in when I walked out, talking on the phone. Maybe that is why I did not hear anything. While explaining things on the phone, I sat in the car."

"That makes some sense, and you have the call record to collaborate? You did format your phone."

"I have it backed up. I can share it with you."

"Did father agree to drop Paulo as a client because I am told he is overseas now?"

"No, I am sure he did not. The stubborn guy that he was, he did not agree, nor did he tell me anything, despite me asking him repeatedly. I miss him, Charles. I really do," said Cliff as he covered his face and started weeping. "He was the only thing close to a family I had. You tell me, why would I want him dead? He gave me everything and took nothing in return. He took nothing from me, never interfered, and always looked after me."

"That's what I keep hearing from everyone I meet. Then, why was he shot? There must have been something that we were all missing. He must have hurt someone."

"All I know is that Paulo's 'case' involved a lot of money—millions. It had something to do with a lot of money. Honestly, things Paulo is into—drugs, counterfeits, conflict diamonds—you name it, he does it. He needs people to move things around, if you know what I mean."

"No, that's too far, Uncle Cliff. You know how principled father was. He would never get into all that. At best, he represented him."

"Yeah, you are right. I am just too scared—scared for my life. I don't know what might happen next. Even I could be on the list. One tends to think of the worst."

"Was there anyone else in the room? Did you notice anything different?"

"No, no one, not even Andy, was called. We had a short meeting. Nothing.. Same old library, same old Robert. A few books here and there moved from the shelf, nothing out of the ordinary."

"Yeah, I know. We saw the footage of you leaving at the same time the shot was fired. Don't worry, I know your story now, Uncle Cliff, but you have to meet the captain and tell them your story. You are still a suspect, you know the drill."

"I know, Charles, but I never thought I would be on the opposite side."

"You have to understand that we are trying to find the killer before he attacks any of my family members again. This time, he might not miss at all. Talk to the captain."

Cliff hesitated but eventually agreed, "Talk to the captain, Uncle Cliff, please. That is your best choice right now. Maybe if he is convinced, he can put you under protective custody until things get over and the killer is caught."

"It has to be Paulo. He must have wanted something from Robert, and Robert must have refused. He must have shot him for that."

"He came before you, Uncle Cliff, in the day, and he left much before you, and nothing happened until late in the evening. Plus, he is out of our jurisdiction now anyway. He must have fled after the murder."

"Paulo would never get his hands dirty. He would have sent someone later when he had an alibi. These mob bosses don't do things on their own. He would have first left the jurisdiction and then ordered his execution. Have you found anything yet? Any leads?"

"Nothing yet, not even a single lead. Actually, we were hoping maybe you could help, but it seems even you don't know anything about Paulo and his transactions."

"What about the crime scene? Anything there?"

"Just an empty bullet casing and a cufflink, the one father gave all of us, remember?"

"I know I still have mine and wear it occasionally, especially when we achieve something important in the firm."

"What's the point, Uncle Cliff? Anyone and everyone has them. It's not as if they were rare."

"First of all, it was a gift from your father. Rare or not, it was unique. Treasure it. And second, you may not know this, but when we placed an order for the cufflinks for everyone, four were made differently."

"What? Different? What do you mean?"

"What I mean is, mine, yours, and Darcy's cufflinks, along with Robert's, are made of platinum—more precious, stronger, and not easily broken. Whereas the ones given to everyone else are made of silver. Robert had them polished in such a way that they looked like silver. You know how he was, never wanting anyone to know the difference. He wanted everyone to feel equal but, at the same time, let the people he loved the most know they were special to him."

Charles sighed, "Father and his mysterious ways. He always loved a good secret and a good mystery, hiding things in plain sight. There, yet always hidden. He loved the feeling of secrecy. Even his death has become a bigger mystery than what we can solve. Alright, Uncle Cliff, if you remember anything more, anything at all, you know how to reach me," (hands him his phone found in the lodge), "and stop being scared."

Charles called Captain Nate.

"Hey, Cap, yeah, I am fine. I know it's late, but I can't wait till morning. I found Cliff. He is here with me at his lodge. He is fine. He is a bit scared, though, with all that is happening. I have asked him to meet you and give his statement. Send a patrol car to pick him up. I don't want him driving alone. Alright, take care."

"All done, Uncle. Be safe and be in touch. A police escort is on its way to take you to the station and to a safe house, if need be. Until then, stay indoors. Let's not take any chances now."

"I hope you find this asshole soon, Charles. And if you do, I swear I'll shoot him. He took away everything from me."

Charles smiled. "Get in line, Uncle. Everyone I meet wants to kill the shooter. The problem is, I can't find him." Charles walked to his car, got in, and drove off.

While driving, he kept thinking, What is it that he is missing in all of this? The killer had some reason to come back again. His face grew angry with frustration and guilt. Why is this taking so much time? I am a detective and am not able to solve my own father's case. It's been days, and I don't even have one solid piece of evidence.

Charles reached home late and saw Darcy outside on the terrace. The barbecue was lit, giving out a lot of smoke. "Oh, shit! The barbecue."

He went into the mansion and saw Lisa waiting. The anger could be seen on her face. "Where were you? I have been waiting for you."

"I will explain everything. Let's go up. Darcy is waiting too."

They both climb up to the terrace. On the terrace, they saw Darcy working on the laptop, struggling with something. "What's wrong, Darcy? Need help?"

Darcy set the laptop aside.

"Finally!! Look who decided to show up! I got this barbecue going half an hour ago. I thought you were not coming. No help is needed with the laptop, thanks. Went to the bank today, like I told you. They want some papers. I'm just looking for them."

"I'm sorry I got late. I had a lot to do today. Are you sure about the laptop? Do you want me or Lisa to help you?" "Naah... not that important. I'll try on my other computer, it's all backed up," she kept the laptop behind her.

"Okay," nodded Charles. "What are we having for dinner?" Darcy pointed to the burgers and beer on the table. Charles picked up the plate and sat at the table. Lisa filled her plate. "If you don't mind, can I take this to my room? I am really tired."

"Sure," responded Darcy and Charles.

"How was your day, Charles? Anything important? Any progress?"

"Yeah, big time. Found Cliff."

"You did?" exclaimed Darcy. "Where? How? Did the bastard confess to the crime? Did you arrest him?"

"Let me explain, will you, Darcy? God, I keep the detective aside at home. Will you keep the executioner aside for a minute?"

"Sorry, Charles.. Go on, I get impatient because I want the killer caught as soon as possible."

"We all do, Darcy. We spoke to him. He said he came to meet father to tell him to be cautious about Paulo, that is all. He said he loved him and would never want him dead. He gave Cliff everything. He walked out calmly because he was on a call and had never heard the gunshot. If he had heard it, he would have definitely gone back inside to check."

"Crap, all crap. I'm telling you, Charles, he is lying. There has to be something more. He was the only one there."

"For now, we cannot be sure. But I feel he is not lying. Just relax and give it time. Plus, we have him in custody. He is not going anywhere till we solve it."

"Then that leaves us with only one person remaining, Paulo."

"There is a good chance he is behind all this, but he is not in the country right now, and we are trying to locate him. God knows when that will happen. Well, at least Cliff is out of the picture, one less variable to worry about."

"I wanted this barbecue to be our family time, you know, like the old days with my father. I wanted to spend some time together relaxing and drinking. You have had such a busy day, and Lisa is already tired and in her room."

"Things were just out of my control today. Let me make it up for today. We should go out for dinner tomorrow, just the three of us, to relax and enjoy like you wanted today."

"I understand, Charles. Getting Cliff was a big achievement. Let's go to our father's favourite place for steak."

Charles smiled in agreement, and Darcy doused the barbecue. They both headed down to their rooms. Charles went into his room and Lisa was already in bed.

"Hi handsome, I was waiting for you. I slipped into something to make you smile."

Lisa stepped out from under the covers, wearing seductive lingerie. Charles walked up to her and pulled her close. "God, I needed this. You look like an angel. I thought you were tired."

"I will be if you keep talking, Detective."

He kissed her on the lips and pulled her into bed.

The next morning, Andy knocked on the door and said, "Breakfast is ready, Master Charles."

"Be right there," Charles retorted with a frustrated tone. "It makes me feel like a little boy."

Charles turned around to see Lisa lying next to him and said, "You are a sight for sore eyes. I can't tell you how much I love you."

Lisa kissed him. "I love you too, baby. Let's get dressed and have breakfast."

"We will after some time. I have work to finish," he pulled her back in the covers, and Lisa was heard laughing loudly.

They both got dressed in their morning gowns and came down for breakfast.

"Good morning, sleepyheads. I see someone is still tired from last night."

"Good morning, Darcy," both of them greeted her.

Lisa smiled as Darcy picked up the hint of what happened.

"You have to try these, Lisa. Andy makes the best egg Benedict in the world."

"I will take you up on that. I am famished."

"Famished, my my, what have you been up to?" smiled Darcy.

"Are we still going for dinner tonight, Charles?"

"Dinner?" asked Lisa.

Charles turned to Darcy and said, "Yes, we are definitely going. I'm sorry for ruining last night," and then turned back to Lisa, "Yes, Lisa, I asked Darcy last night but forgot to mention it to you. Completely slipped my mind. I wanted to make up for being late."

"But is it safe, Charles? You know I was shot at," said Lisa with a trembling tone.

"Don't worry at all, Lisa. I understand your fear. We will have a police car escorting us the whole time."

"I trust you, Charles, but you have to understand my concern. I have a genuine reason to be scared."

"We understand completely, Lisa. If something does happen, I'll jump in front of you this time," smiled Darcy.

"That is sweet of you, Darcy, but I just might take you up on that," laughed Lisa.

"Let me take care of the bookings this time. If I leave it to Charles, he will forget that too."

Charles looked at Darcy with a funny expression and rolled his eyes. "Will not."

"We understand completely Lisa. If something does happen, I'll jump in front of you this time," smiled Darcy.

"That is sweet of you, Darcy, but I just might take you up on that," laughed Lisa.

"Let me take care of the bookings this time. If I leave it to Charles, he will forget that too."

Charles looked at Darcy with a funny expression and rolled his eyes. "Will not."

Chapter 5

Mr. Grey

While they were eating breakfast, chatting, and laughing, the bell rang.

"Andy, will you get that? See who it is," asked Darcy.

Andy walked to the front door to open it, and a person in a black suit entered the mansion. He spoke to Andy about something and then walked into the dining area where they were sitting.

"You must be Charles. I assume Andy opened the door, and you, Darcy," he then turned to Lisa. "You, I don't know," he said politely.

"Since you came to see us at our house, shouldn't you be the one introducing yourself first, Mr....?" asked Lisa.

"Grey," he replied.

"I am Robert's lawyer."

"Do lawyers also need lawyers?" quipped Lisa.

"Yes, they do," Grey replied in a bland tone.

Lisa turned to Charles and whispered, "Not a chatty one, is he?"

"How can we help you, Mr. Grey?" asked Darcy as she got up to shake his hand.

"Well, I hope I am not disturbing your personal time, but this is urgent and it cannot be made into an evening jacket event."

Mr. Grey pulled out a sealed envelope from his briefcase, showed it to them, and put it on the table.

"In my custody, I have your father's last and final will. Please accept my condolences for the departed soul. I never thought the day would come so soon. He was a dear friend. This will is to be opened and read after his death in front of both his children and his butler together. I apologise in advance, but if Miss" (points at Lisa) "...can leave the room, we begin."

"Miss Lisa is not going anywhere," said Charles.

"She is family, she stays," exclaimed Darcy.

"Well, that is your choice. If you feel the need to have an audience other than you three, whoever you wish to disclose the contents of this will is your choice."

"Father made a will. When was this?"

"About 3 years ago, he came to me and said life is short, it's better to be prepared. You know how he was, no one understood what he was thinking. Maybe that is why he was so good at what he did."

Grey put aside his briefcase and picked up the sealed envelope again. He then broke open the seal. He pulled out a few papers with stamps on them and started reading them line-by-line.

"This is the last and final will of Robert Knight, and he has stated the following with a sound mind, without coercion, and free consent to be executed upon his death.

All his immovable properties are given to his two children and can be divided by them as they deem fit. If the need arises, they can sell the properties, except for this mansion, which he also leaves in the name of his children, but this cannot be sold by them during their lifetime. After their lifetime, the mansion should be converted into a home for children with special needs. The necessary arrangements can be made with the government by my children.

Andy will, at all times, and if he so agrees, take care of the mansion. For this, he will have the right to live in this mansion till he deems fit, for which he shall be paid by my children out of my income. He has also left this one book to Andy (showing the description to Andy). He said it is in the study on the bookshelf. Can you get it, Andy?"

"Yes, Mr. Grey," said Andy as he saw the description. "I will be right back with it. It's on Master Robert's desk." A few minutes later, he came back with the book and handed it to Mr. Grey. He put it on the table before him and clicked on a photo of it.

Darcy picked it up and flipped the pages, "Nothing special."

Charles took the book and examined it too. "It seems like it was signed by the author. Maybe that's the special part."

"Could be," shrugged Grey as if he were not interested.

"He leaves all his movable property again to his children, including the amount of one million kept in his bank. 'My children are free to divide everything as they deem fit. All I ask is that they do it lovingly and not fight for it.'"

"One million, that's it?" intruded Andy in shock as Mr. Grey paused. "Sorry for my intrusion, sir, but Master Robert must have had more."

"Andy! Why would he hide it?" said Charles.

"I don't mean he is hiding it, sir. I meant the life he lived, the mansion, the suits, and the firm. I thought he must have had more. He pays me and other house staff as well. Did he spend it all on keeping us happy?"

"You know, now that you mentioned it, even Cliff said the same thing: father made millions otherwise and didn't need Paulo in his list of clients. Maybe he gave most of it away to keep everyone satisfied."

Mr. Grey replied, "Well, sometimes clients do not follow the full disclosure rule for the will. I don't know what they gain from that. After death, what good is your money if you keep it hidden? To me, this is all that was disclosed, and more or less that is the main operative part and nothing more. You both can have a look and then I can take it for further action. The list of properties is in Schedule A, which is to be divided as you deem fit."

"Assuming he wanted to hide his money, why would his father hide the money from us, his own children? This baffles me."

"I agree with Mr. Grey on this. What would he get by hiding it from his own children?" said Darcy.

Both Charles and Darcy took the will and started reading it.

Lisa asked Mr. Grey, "Would you like some coffee?"

"No, dear, I must get going. Lawyers hired by lawyers need to work extra hard." He handed a copy of the will to Charles. "Here, you can keep this. I need the original for a few days and for a few legal formalities. I will bring it back when done. You can also photograph the original until then."

Charles got up and clicked photos of the entire will and shared them with Darcy.

Mr. Grey took the will and put it back in his bag. "Good day to you all. I'll see you later."

Mr. Grey leaves the mansion.

"Not one day, not one that does not bring in a surprise. I don't know (Darcy starts sobbing). It's all too much, you know. Ever since father left us, we have not had one day of peace."

Charles got up and hugged Darcy. Lisa also hugged Darcy and said, "It will get better soon. Don't you worry. We are all here with you, and Charles is doing his best to find whoever destroyed our lives like this."

Darcy wiped her tears. "I am okay." Still weeping, she went to the fridge to get a bottle of water. "I will be okay."

Everyone stood in silence for some time, thinking.

"Let's have a great dinner tonight. One last hoorah for father. Try to be positive and forget about all this. What say?"

"Yes! Let's do it," they both replied.

"Okay, then let's finish reading through this will and see what is to be done," said Charles.

"Well, nothing much changes anyway, according to this. It's like he wanted us to continue the same way after his death. In a way, it feels good, you know, finally something that remains still in all the chaos."

"Well, I think we should just take a break and be home today."

"I have an idea. Let's watch a movie," said Lisa.

"You guys go ahead. I have some paperwork to get to the station," said Charles.

"Oh, come on, you boring old cop!" smiled Lisa.

"Give me some time. I will come back soon."

Both Lisa and Darcy headed up to the room, and Charles headed toward his father's study. Charles skipped a beat. "I never thought coming back to this room would be so difficult. Nothing is the same without you, father. If only I was as brilliant as you, I would have understood what happened here. I am stuck. I have nothing."

Andy entered the study. "I hope you all enjoy the dinner. You deserve it after all that has been going on. I have still not found anything of use in his papers, Master Charles."

"Well, keep looking then, please."

Andy left, agreeing with Charles.

Chapter 6

The Last Dinner

Day turned to evening, and Charles was so mesmerised by work that he didn't realise the time. Going through the evidence again and again, he sat at his father's computer, staring through folders desperately to find something, hanging on in the hope of finding a sliver of proof. "Something at least, father. What were you trying to tell me? What am I not picking up?" He kept scrolling through files and files.

Darcy entered the room. "You already look like he's working so seriously," she said, pointing at Robert's portrait in the study. "God, my eyes go moist every time I see him there. I can't believe he is gone. Get dressed, please. Let's not be late."

"Yes, yes, sorry, I didn't realise the time. It's just that... I am getting desperate now, Darcy. There has to be something that we are overlooking."

"I agree with you, brother," Darcy said as she showed him the watch and gestured with her eyes to get moving.

Charles stretched and went up to his room to get dressed. Lisa was on her way down. "Are you on time ever, Mr. Detective?"

"Five minutes," Charles responded, fastening his pace to get ready. Later, all three of them met in the dining room and stepped out together. Charles faced more heat from the ladies for missing the movie and being late, but there was a general tone of ease in the conversation.

They got in the car and drove off, with a patrol car following them from a distance. They crossed a beautiful lake on the way.

"I have always loved this lake. It's my favourite spot. See, Lisa," Darcy pointed out.

"It looks really beautiful. I would love to see it sometime, once all of this settles down," Lisa said.

They drove by the lake and further into town.

"There, that's where we are having dinner," Darcy pointed out. "We used to come here a lot with mom and dad."

"Wow! It looks fancy," Lisa exclaimed, her face lighting up. The foodie in her was elated. They all got out of the car and headed for the restaurant. The police escort stopped behind them, signalling to Charles that they would be in the car, keeping an eye out.

"Do you have a reservation?" the manager at the desk asked.

All of them start laughing. Lisa stared with a blank look, trying to realise what happened.

"Hey, Uncle, how have you been?" Charles greeted the manager.

"Fat and growing," the manager replied, laughing.

After a few moments, he stopped laughing. "I am sorry about what happened, Charles. I never thought anyone would do that to Robert. He never hurt a soul. God bless him," he said with empathy.

"That is what we are also trying to comprehend," said Darcy.

"The usual table then, and who may I ask, is this lovely lady?" the manager inquired.

"That's Lisa," Charles replied.

"Really, her! With you? How is that? Is she blind?" the manager joked.

"Come on, Uncle, give me some credit," Charles chuckled.

"Lovely to meet you, Lisa. You have a good eye, Charles. I will give you that. I can't say the same for Lisa. Be careful with this one, Lisa. Unlike his father, he only knows how to work," the manager said teasingly.

"Right on the money with that one. You have to beg him for time," Lisa replied with a big smile on her face.

"So then, two steaks and Lisa, what would you like to have?" Both nodded in agreement.

"I'll go with them on this one. So, three steaks," Lisa decided.

The manager took them to their usual table at the back and then went to the kitchen to place the order. After some time, the steak was served by the waiter along with a nice bottle of wine. All three were seen smiling and enjoying their food and drinking their wine.

Lisa looked up and, while chatting with Charles, happened to glance at the window behind him. She saw someone lurking outside the restaurant, hiding and looking in from the side of the window, trying to keep himself hidden in the shadows. Her expression changed starkly to a very scared look, as if something spooked her. Her face went pale, and she started sweating.

Darcy noticed the change and asked, “Lisa, what’s wrong?”

“I saw someone at the window peeking inside. I got frightened by him.”

Darcy leaned towards her and said, “But I don’t see anyone. Do you, Charles?”

“No, nothing,” Charles responded.

Lisa rubbed her eyes, saying, “Maybe it’s me. Maybe I am still shaken up. It’s not every day that you get shot at,” in a humorous tone.

“Let me go out and check once. Will that relax you?” Charles offered.

“No, let it be, Charles. Not required. Let’s just enjoy the dinner. Sorry, I got you both worried for nothing,” Lisa replied.

"Wait, let me. We are here for a nice dinner and to relax—one night of peace. I don't want you or Darcy to be slightly troubled. I want smiles all around," Charles insisted.

Charles got up and walked to the window, saw no one, then walked outside the restaurant and looked around. He saw no one unusual in sight, no one at the window either. Just normal people walking around and talking.

Before going back in, he decided to have a look in the alley as well, just to be absolutely sure. While walking to it, he heard a sound. He looked around in the alley and saw the shadow of a man moving towards the restaurant.

Charles decided to follow the person slowly because of the preceding events that had shaken the family. He saw him wearing a black jacket. "It's him," Charles realised. He was absolutely sure. He was the guy they saw jumping over the fence.

The person entered the restaurant from the back door, then turned around and gave a sinister smile to Charles, as if mocking him, and then locked the door before he could enter. Charles shook the door, but it wouldn't open. He ran back to the front entrance of the restaurant to warn the girls of the danger they were in.

The restaurant was almost empty. He ran inside and said, "He is here. Take cover."

The girls didn't understand what was happening. They just looked at him, confused, trying to understand what he was saying.

"What's wrong, Charles? Who is here?" Darcy asked.

"The killer is here. I'm not letting him get away this time, no matter what. Take cover."

"Shit!! Let's go," Darcy responded.

Charles called the captain and explained everything to him.

"We are coming, Charles. Don't be a hero. He won't get away this time. Protect the girls first. You have a backup. Let them help, and get out immediately," the captain instructed.

"Not letting him get away this time, Captain."

A gunshot was heard. "Get behind me!" shouted Charles.

Darcy asked Lisa to help her overturn the table, and they both took cover behind it. Charles told the manager to hide.

"It's him, the guy who tried to shoot me. He is back to finish what he started," Charles explained.

Hearing the gunshot, the deputies also came. More backup was on its way, along with the captain.

Lisa started crying and shivering in fear. "He is here for me, Charles. He will kill me this time. Oh God, God…"

"It will be okay. Trust me, Lisa. I won't let anything happen to either of you this time."

"This is between me and him. Hold her, Darcy. I will finish this today once and for all. Stay here only. I don't want to make it easy for him. Be out of the line of fire," Charles directed.

"Let the deputies do their job, Charles. Stay behind the table. We are safe here," Darcy said in a suppressed yet angry tone.

"I have to. I can't let him get away, not this time," Charles insisted.

Charles slid out from behind the table and signalled the deputies to cover him. He turned around the wall, going further in towards the kitchen. Both the deputies followed him.

A shot was fired again, and it hit one of the deputies in the head. He fell flat on the floor. Seeing the accuracy of the shooter, Charles shuddered and rethought his strategy.

"Take cover," Charles said loudly, "and move back. No one comes out till I say."

Charles waved to the other policeman that he could not see the shooter. He would keep an eye while the policeman could help the civilians escape. Realising this was a small window to escape, the few who were in front of the restaurant, including the manager, ran out the door, keeping their heads low, while the deputy helped them move quickly. Some people, including the girls, remained.

Another shot was fired as the shooter noticed all the chaos and movements. Suddenly, everything went still. Charles fired back to scare the shooter. Lisa and Darcy were still behind the table around the wall. Lisa was now trembling with fear and frozen, not able to move. The entrance was far for them to run to. They stayed there, knowing they couldn't get out without getting in the line of fire. They would only make the killer's life easier by doing it.

Charles again signalled the deputy to cover him. He went in firing this time, further ahead. The second deputy followed him in, walking along the walls. Shots were fired again, but both Charles and the policeman took cover, and no one was hurt.

Charles signalled the deputy, asking him to go around while he went from this side. Charles fired a few rounds, giving time to the second deputy to escape and came in from the back entrance. He emptied his clip, discarded it, and reloaded.

A shot was heard from the backside. It was the second deputy who broke the lock. Hearing this, Charles was shocked. "Not that loud, you rookie. He will kill you for sure."

Charles knew now he had to act fast since the killer must have heard the sound too and realised what was happening. Multiple shots were fired. Charles decided to take a chance. It was now or never. What if the killer shot the other deputy and escaped again? Charles could not let that happen a third time.

He knew this killer kept coming back to finish the job, and he was good at it. He followed them here without being noticed by the patrol car and also evaded getting caught until now. It was imperative that he be caught and caught alive. He was the last lead in the case. Without him, the trail would go cold, and Charles would never be able to find out who killed his father.

Charles fired a round in the air to confuse the killer and then threw some cutlery on the floor opposite him. Charles then sprinted to the back of the kitchen, where the other entry was. The back door was open, and there were many shots fired, but no casualties could be seen. Charles grunted in frustration. "No, not again. He got away."

Charles slowly moved to the back, planting every foot carefully. No one could be seen. He then leaned against the door to look out, and he saw the other deputy outside in the alley. Seeing Charles' head pop out, the deputy immediately fired.

"It's me," said Charles. "Hold your fire, you goddamn trigger-happy rookie. See before you shoot."

"Sorry," he replied while raising both his hands.

"Did you see him run?" asked Charles.

"No one came from this end. I heard shots and thought it's better to fall back and wait to see if he comes out. There was no way for me to be sure who shot who."

Charles realised that if the killer had not left the building from the back, he was still hiding inside. The girls were inside too. Charles quickly ran back to them. At the end of the kitchen, he heard a slight sound. Charles paused to understand what it was. He turned around, and there was a gun firmly pointing to his head.

It was him. It was the killer. The moment froze. He knew this was his end, and the killer got him. With the gun to his head, he was worried for Darcy and Lisa. The killer would surely go after them and finish the job.

He gestured to Charles to drop his weapon. Charles had no choice but to comply. Charles slowly lowered his gun and put it on the floor. "Where is the goddamn backup when you need it?" thought Charles.

He turned around and saw his face, a long moustache and a rugged beard, a tattoo on both his arms, and a big scar on his forehead, as if someone had cut it in half. Charles could see his death. The stare of the killer was stone cold.

The killer stayed silent. Charles mustered up the courage and said to him, "Kill me, but leave them out of this." The killer didn't even flinch. Charles knew he was a professional and would not stop until all targets were executed.

Sirens were heard outside as the police vehicles approached. After a few moments, while Charles and the killer stand face-to-face, the captain on the loudspeaker said, "You are surrounded. Come out with your hands in the air, and no one will get hurt. Surrender yourself."

"Hear that? Even if you kill me, you still have nowhere to go. This place is surrounded," Charles warned.

The killer looked around very calmly. "Audite," said the killer in a heavy, husky voice.

They heard footsteps at the back door. It was the police, for sure. The killer had nowhere to go now.

The killer quickly grabbed Charles, turned him around, and put the gun to the back of his head. He started to push himself to walk. They both walked slowly. They went around the corner and back to the front part of the restaurant, where the seating was.

They were visible to the police now and also to Lisa and Darcy. They stopped right there, just before the end of the wall. The killer was smart. He used Charles as his shield and stayed behind the wall, so the police could not shoot or ambush him.

He was trained, there was no doubt about it. Charles was thinking, he knows what he is doing, keeping me hostage. But how do I get out of this? One wrong move and I could be killed, or he could be fired at. I have to be very smart about this. I need him alive to know who is behind all of this.

Seeing them, Lisa screamed, "Leave him. Please, please, let him live."

"Save him!" shouted Darcy to the captain outside.

The captain responded on the loudspeaker, "There is no need for this. Drop your weapon and step out. We will not harm you. There is no way to escape for you, surrender now. No one has to get hurt."

The killer again mumbled something in a heavy, husky voice.

"What? What are you saying?" responded Charles, unable to understand.

The killer tightened his grip on Charles to keep him from moving too much.

Darcy saw a gun on the floor in the hand of the deputy, who was shot earlier by the killer. She decided to help and handed it to Charles. While hearing the killer mumble something, Charles happened to glance at Darcy's movement. She pointed to the gun with her eyes. He understood what she was staring at and immediately realised what she was trying to do. Scared, he signalled Darcy to stop by blinking his eyes slowly. He knew the killer would not miss this and would shoot her the moment he saw any movement.

Lisa tried to stop Darcy from crying and held her hand. Something had to be done, but Darcy did not listen and wanted to save her brother. The captain, seeing this from outside, also realised what was happening and signalled his squad to be ready.

Charles again signalled Darcy with his eyes to stop. "I need him alive at all costs," thought Charles. All of this was happening so fast. No one was in their right mind to think of the consequences.

Charles thought, "No one understood the importance of this man being caught alive. Where would he run anyway? Even if he kills me, he is surrounded. He is using me as a hostage to escape, so he won't kill me until he is absolutely sure he cannot escape. I have some time."

Charles understood that the killer was holding a gun to his head, and even if the police shot the killer, the killer would still be able to kill him before getting hit. As a professional, he would shoot Charles and also use his body as a shield. He would not give up easily and would go down fighting. The only way to keep him alive was if, somehow, Charles managed to capture him. He had to find out why he was doing this.

He decided to go for it and take a chance to try to keep the killer alive. He signalled Darcy to throw the gun at him with his eyes while the killer was looking at the deputies outside and assessing his situation.

Darcy understood and decided to go towards the gun. Charles wanted to do this quickly while the killer was distracted by the police force outside the restaurant.

Charles signalled Darcy to wait and further gestured to go together. Darcy blinked in agreement. With his fingers, he counted: one, two, three.

Charles lifted the killer's hand up and punched him. He then bent down to get out of the line of shooting of the killer and sprang forward to catch the gun from Darcy.

Darcy leaped out from behind the table towards the dead body of the policeman to throw the gun at Charles. The killer came to him and realised what was happening. He quickly turned the gun downward to shoot Charles.

"BANG"

Everything paused. No one realised what happened. Charles lay on the floor, unmoving, with Darcy standing in front of him, holding the gun. Lisa watched from behind the table, trying to comprehend the swift turn of events.

The killer, standing tall with his gun pointing at Charles, suddenly fell to his knees. He had been shot. The bullet went right through his throat, and volumes of blood started squirting out.

Darcy realised there was no time to throw the gun at Charles, so she made a split-second decision and shot the killer. Charles, now on his feet, rushed to the killer to stop the bleeding, shouting for paramedics and help. The captain came running inside, responding to the commotion.

Darcy fell back on the floor, dropping the gun. Charles put his hand on the killer's throat, but the man choked on his own blood and stopped breathing. Charles turned around angrily towards Darcy, accusing her of shooting the only lead they had to find out who killed their father.

"Are you mad, Charles? Have you lost all your senses?" Darcy shouted back, weeping. "He was going to shoot you, damned! Your back was towards him. By the time I would have thrown the gun at you, he would have gotten you. I made a decision in that split second. I had to save you. I was not thinking of what would happen. I could not lose you too. I just fired, and it hit him.

"You could have shot him in the leg at least."

"I am not a trained shooter, Charles. It just fired. I was not aiming at his neck or anything in particular."

Charles turned around in frustration and saw the killer's dead body. "He is gone, it's over. Now I have no way to catch my father's killer."

Lisa stepped out from behind the table and walked up to Charles. "She didn't have a choice, Charles. You have to understand that she is your sister. She did it for you. I could not move. At least she had the guts to do this. I would have done the same thing."

The captain approached Darcy with a bottle of water, trying to console her. He then picked up the gun and handed it to his deputy.

"It's okay. You are okay now, Darcy. It's over. Take her outside and get her examined," he told the deputy. "Easy now, Darcy, let's go."

He then walked to Charles, who was infuriated.

"Charles," he said calmly, "listen to me."

"Don't, Captain, don't even start."

"Charles, had you been in her shoes, you would have done the exact same thing to save your sister. What if the killer had her and you had to shoot? Would you have done anything else? Would you have thought to save your sister or the killer just because you wanted some answers? She risked her life for you. It was a choice between a dead killer and a dead brother. Think about it. It was a simple choice."

Charles leaned against the wall and slid down. He then held his head and just sat there for a moment.

"He was the only lead I had, Captain, the last of it. Without him, I have nothing—no case, nothing. Now I will never find out why he killed my father or why he came back for me. He was following someone's orders, and that person is still out there."

"Is that all you think of, Charles? Just for once, think about your sister and your girlfriend. Think of what they are going through for you. Lisa was shot at for you. She is still with you, and Darcy saved you. Still, all you can think of is the damn killer and your selfish reasons to save him."

"I loved my father and looked up to him every day, and I miss him even more. I loved him, Captain. He was my idol and my hero. Do you understand the feeling? I failed my hero. I can't even find his killer, and everywhere I try to look, it's just dead ends and dead bodies. I failed him. What good am I if I cannot get justice for my father? A fraud and a useless detective."

"All I know is that right now, your family needs you. Whatever little you have left, they need you. Just look at them, just see what state they are in."

The captain helped Charles get up. Charles saw Darcy outside at the back of the ambulance and walked up to her. Lisa was sitting with her. They both looked at him with anger. He realised his mistake and the blame he threw around. He lashed out at Darcy without thinking.

"I am sorry. I really am. I let you both down. I put you both in harm's way again."

Darcy looked at him and did not respond. Lisa opened her arms and hugged Darcy and Charles.

"We are okay. That's what matters most. Plus, we don't need you to babysit us. We can take care of ourselves. I feel safer with Darcy now."

The captain walked up to Charles.

"We found the gun on him. Only 1 round left."

"Is it?"

"Yes, it's a Magnum, but I have still sent it to forensics to be absolutely sure. We can't make any more mistakes now. I think you guys are safe now. The killer is dead, and I don't see any more threats. Try to be at ease now. I'll keep security at your mansion for some more time, just in case."

"Safe? You call this safe? I am scared to ask even what you call danger," retorted Darcy angrily. "What about Paulo? He is still out there. He will just send another one of his killers after us."

"We still haven't located him, but we are on it. Go home and rest now. Let's look at this in the morning while the forensics do their work at night."

"No one is safe, Captain. They follow us everywhere, every time," said Charles.

"I understand your fear. I would have been scared too, had it been me. Darcy, I'll need your statement tomorrow."

"As you say, Captain, What else are we here for? We do your work and give you statements for it," replied Darcy in frustration.

The captain did not respond. He understood she was angry. He took Charles aside.

"Did he say anything while you were his hostage? Why is he after you? Why did he kill Robert? He held you for a long time. If he wanted to just shoot you, he could have left from the back before we even came in."

"He could have, but he wanted a hostage because he knew he could not escape without one. Plus, the deputy had reached the back door before he could escape."

"Think, Charles. Did he say anything at all?"

"No, I don't think he spoke English. He just said one weird word in another language, 'audii'... 'audii' something, I don't know. I don't think it's of much relevance. Maybe I heard it wrong."

"Audii? Was he talking about his car? Maybe he wants us to look into his car."

"Is there a vehicle outside? Maybe we will find something there."

"No, there is no suspicious vehicle parked outside. Are you sure he didn't say anything else?"

"Absolutely sure. I am in my senses, Captain," said Charles with an attitude.

"Okay, Mr. I am in my senses, go home, get some rest, and come to the station tomorrow. Drop the wise-ass attitude when you come. It does not help."

Charles walked off to his car. Lisa and Darcy were already in the back seat. Darcy had her head on Lisa's shoulder, and her eyes were closed.

They all drove back to the mansion.

"I am sorry, Darcy. I really am. I got caught up with the wrong idea and did not realise what you did for me. I feel bad that we can't even have one meal without it turning into a disaster, not once. What has our life come to?"

"Please just let it go, Charles. We are all fine. Let's just go rest. Finally, the killer is dead," said Lisa. Darcy did not open her eyes or respond.

They drove up to the mansion. The police parked their cars outside for night patrols. They went inside and into their own rooms. They changed and got into bed. Lisa tucked in Darcy, and her light went off. Lisa and Charles were in bed. Charles was staring at the ceiling.

"I can't sleep, Lisa."

"What's wrong, hon? Try to talk about it."

"This is the third attempt. I could have been killed today. I was scared for my life. Any moment today, it could have been over."

"Try and breathe. Stay calm. I can feel your pain. I was shot at too. It's frightening. Give it time, it heals all wounds."

"The situation is just getting more and more intense, Lisa."

"You know, Charles, you are right. Ever since your father, everything has been spiralling down and looping around. Even I am astonished. Every time we find a lead, it turns into a dead end. I just can't fathom what kind of ongoing killing spree this is. We are all in grave danger, and it just doesn't seem to end. It just keeps getting tougher by the day to survive. In full honesty, Charles, even I am scared of what we have gotten into."

"Come on, Lisa, are you having second thoughts about us?"

"God no, Charles, I love you. You know that. I could have left the day I was shot, but I did not. I chose to be with you. Doesn't that tell you how much I care for you? But yes, any other girl would have had second thoughts. Too bad you are too good-looking for me to leave you for someone else," smiled Lisa. "You cannot survive a day without me."

"I'm sorry. I didn't mean to hurt you," said Charles as he hugged her tightly.

Someone knocked at the door and said, "It's Darcy. Sorry to disturb you. Are you still up?"

"I can't sleep, can you?" asked Lisa. "We were missing you anyway. Glad that you came."

"Not a wink. Just too scared now to be alone. Is it okay if I join you two? I don't feel like being alone tonight. I killed a person today, and I feel broken and jittery."

"Of course, love, you don't even have to ask. Come here."

Darcy lay down on Lisa's side, weeping, "I feel like an emotional wreck."

"I was telling Charles the same thing. I understand this feeling. We all have gone through a severe trauma now, and we are together in this. We will fight through."

"Just try to get some shut-eye. We had a tough day today. Tomorrow will be better. Time is a great healer."

She switched off the side lamp. "Goodnight."

"Goodnight," they both responded. Lisa held on to Darcy.

Darcy could not sleep the whole night and kept turning. She could not stop thinking about killing a person. But she had to do it, she had to save her brother. Still, it was a human life she took for the price she paid. Charles noticed her tossing and turning but kept quiet. He knew nothing could console her.

The next morning, Charles opened his eyes to see Lisa next to him, but Darcy was not there. He sat up to get a better view, but she was not in the room. He stretched and decided to go to her room to check if she was doing okay.

Just then, Darcy entered the room with breakfast, along with Andy. "Rise and shine, you two. A new day, a new beginning. I am not letting anyone or anything ruin today."

"Good morning, Darcy." Charles was happy to see her up.

"Well, after the shit night we had, I could not sleep the entire night. The mind-boggling thought of killing a person was too much for me. Then I realised that it's sad that we don't have a lead to father's murder, but on the flip side, the shooter who was after us all is finally dead. That gave me some peace of mind and calmness. I felt relaxed. Now I don't have to look over my shoulder every time I walk out or take a police escort every time I even decide to leave the boundary of this mansion."

She then turned to Charles and said, "Charles, my lovely brother, stop blaming yourself, please, for everything. You also have to remember that we can take care of ourselves. You don't have to fight this alone anymore."

Listening to this, both felt calm. The change in expression could be seen on their faces. Charles heard the conversation in silence and nodded.

"You two have been there for me and supported me emotionally through all this, so here's something I cooked for the both of you as a small token of gratitude. I hope you like it."

"It looks yummy, Darcy. Thank you. I think I'll gobble down the whole thing. I am famished."

"I'm sure Andy made it and you just brought it up," teased Charles. "She hasn't cooked a day in her life. Tell me, my dear sister, how do you boil water?"

Darcy threw a pillow at him and said, "I'll kill you, swear to God, today is your end. I'll kill you."

Seeing this, Lisa smiled.

They all finished breakfast. Andy came in to clean. He was amazed at the scene in the room after what they went through last night. It was as if they had gotten used to it and were healing better now. All smiles in the room. There was a sense of calm after so many days. This naturally brought a smile to Andy's face as well.

"It's lovely to see everyone happy, Master Charles, Madam Darcy, and Lisa."

"What can we do, Andy? You cook so well. Thank God, you will stay here with us forever. Keep feeding us your superfood and we can face anything," said Lisa while making a power pose.

"It will be my pleasure to serve you all. I wish Master Robert was here to see you all together like this. This is all he desired when he was alive. I could see it in his eyes. Every time Charles or Darcy would call, his eyes would just light up. This was such a happy mansion, but after Madam passed, he just stopped calling everyone."

"Day by day, Andy, day by day. That's how we will survive this," said Lisa.

"Well, let's get dressed. I have to go down to the station to talk to the captain about last night. You girls need to come as well. It's a tedious task. Let's get it over with quickly."

Lisa, Darcy, and Charles got ready to go to the station. Just as they were about to leave, Andy stopped them.

"Master Charles, when you have time, I wish to talk to you about your father's library and some documents."

"What about it, Andy?"

"It's about the books and his belongings. What is to be done with them?"

"Everything stays as it is, Andy. Everything is too precious for me to part ways with."

"Very well, Master Charles. Nothing changes. I can share the documents with you in the evening."

Andy and Darcy left.

"Well, alone again, my dear Charles," said Lisa in a flirty tone.

"Really, now?" mocked Charles, tapping at his wristwatch.

"Why not? We have about an hour before we need to leave."

"Well, as they say, since ancient times, if you want to succeed, always agree with your woman," smiled Charles.

Lisa took Charles's hand, and they headed towards the shower, dancing. Later, they were both seen getting dressed together—a little kiss here, a little smile there. They walked down to the living room, waved at Andy, and stepped out. The driveway was sparkling clean.

"It must have rained last night," said Charles. "Everything here shines so bright after it rains. The leaves sparkle, and the floor shines."

"It is a lovely mansion, there is no doubt about that. He made it with a lot of love."

"He made it as mom desired. Everything she said was done."

"Look, Darcy's car is still there. She must be getting ready."

They both called out to Darcy.

Darcy stepped out and started walking hurriedly to their car.

"Coming, coming, sorry I am late."

"It's okay, just get in and let's go."

Just then, Darcy's phone rang. She picked it up. "What? When? Okay, okay, I'll be there."

"Now what, Darcy?" asked Charles.

"My friend just called. Her father had a heart attack, and they are rushing him to the hospital. He might need surgery, and they need blood for it. You go ahead, Charles, I'll catch up. Funerals, deaths, and incidents seem to be the ongoing theme," sighed Darcy. "I'll reach for sure by the time you guys are done with your statement."

"Can't you go after the statement?"

"No, it will be too late by then. She is a dear friend and needs my help. The hospital is on the way to the station. Give me an hour, please."

"Alright, Darcy. Please remember that you have to give the statement today at any cost. It's the top priority. It should have been done last night. This relaxation is only because the captain and the team were there."

"I will be there. Promise. Just an hour."

Chapter 7

Back to the Station

Charles and Lisa drove to the station and parked on the side. Lisa entered her name in the logbook, and Charles showed his badge as they both entered. Captain Nate was sitting at the end of the hall and waved at them to come to him. They walked down the hall while the officers on duty waved at Charles, and they entered the captain's cabin.

"Close the door and have a seat, Charles. I have a few things to share. Where is Darcy?"

"On her way, she had to make an urgent stop. It was a genuine emergency. She will be here, for sure, by the time we finish. She knows the importance of being here today."

"Okay, then let's get started. Do you want to go ahead with the statements or hear the updates on the evidence first?"

"The updates, please. Tell me you have something. I feel like a broken record, playing myself again and again. I really need something."

"Well, I have things, but they're all fragments of a story. That's why I wish to share it with you. Maybe you can piece it together and get a better perspective on things."

"Alright, Captain, let's hear it."

Both Charles and Lisa look at the captain anxiously.

"First things first, we have let Cliff go from protective custody since the shooter was killed last night. We asked him this morning if he wanted to stay on, but he also refused. We still asked him to be around and not leave town. Now that the threat is gone, he wants to get back to his life. *The firm is suffering with one partner dead and the other nowhere to be found by clients. I have to stabilise things at the office*, he said."

"That sounds about right. He was genuinely concerned, even when I spoke to him about the murder. It's fine, let him be at peace and do as he wishes. He has suffered enough already."

"Second, we spoke to about twenty people already about the cufflinks gifted by your father."

"Just twenty till now? There must be more."

“There aren’t any more. He mainly gave them out to the people in the firm and to his loved ones, so about twenty of them in total. They all seem to have the pairs with them intact, and they cherish them even more since he passed. They were very possessive about them.”

“Did you know he had four made differently, out of platinum instead of silver?”

“Well, that is a detail I am not privy to. It’s not on the papers either, and it seems you also did not feel the importance of sharing it with me, Charles.”

“I am sorry, Captain, but I thought it was irrelevant. Cliff shared it with me, and I had absolutely no idea about this. Father and his mysterious ways. He enjoyed the thrill of hiding a secret in plain sight. Cliff told me that father had them made specially for himself, Cliff, Darcy, and me, the people closest to him. I did not share it because I don’t think anything turns on it. It’s just one of my father’s little gestures.”

“Well, I guess then nothing changes. Anyway, like I was saying, we spoke to about twenty people. They all have them. Some had the boxes missing, no biggie, but more or less had them in their possession. So we had no reason to question them either. Had even one of them lost a single one, we would have called them in for further questioning.

“But how are you corroborating this, Captain? We don’t even know how many pairs were made and distributed in the first place.”

“We thought of that too, and we traced the cufflinks to the shop that made them on special order. They were not mass-produced. Get this, after the owner passed away due to natural causes, the family shut down the shop and stopped making cufflinks on order. They just went into retail and eventually sold their brand to another. When they could not sustain the business, the new company did not have records of the old one in total, just a few years of it.

We traced the next of kin of the owner, a really old lady in her nineties, living on the outskirts. She could not remember much, but she said that her late husband, until he ran the business, kept everything logged and noted. She also said he was very particular about paying taxes, so he always issued a bill with the quantity and amount to the purchaser. He would never sell a pair without a bill, even if it meant the customer walking away and not buying anything. He was very particular about the material used and the satisfaction of his customers. It was rare that the customers ever came back with a complaint, and if they did, he would change them immediately. He always kept them happy. His quality was impeccable."

"But how did she know about all this, and that too in such vivid details?"

"Exactly my next question to her. She said that being a homemaker, once the kids grew and left, she started helping out at the shop. It was more than helping, it was just for his company. She even showed photographs of herself and her late husband in the shop working together. She would help out with small things like packing and billing, etc., till he passed away. She did not possess the skills to make them."

Just then Charles' phone rang. He cut it. It rang again. Charles put it on hold this time. But then, after a minute, it rang again.

"Will you get that?" said the captain in an irritated tone.

"It's from the mansion. It must be Andy. Can I be excused? It must be important. He never calls like this." Charles got up and went to the side, signalling the captain for a minute.

"This better be important, Andy. I am in the middle of a very important discussion with the captain."

"Master Charles, I wish to share something important with you. It might help with the case," said Andy in a slightly agitated tone.

"Alright, tell me, then, and make it quick, please."

"Not on the phone, Master Charles. It's better if I do it in person."

"We will be home in a few hours after this, Andy. We can talk then."

"I would not have called Master Charles, if this was not urgent. Sorry, you have to understand."

"Why don't you come to the station, then, Andy? We can talk here. It's private and safe."

"That would be better, Master Charles. I will see you there. I am on my way."

"What happened?" asked Lisa.

"Nothing. It was Andy. He said he had something important to discuss that could not wait regarding the case. So I called him to the station since we are all here. So where were we, Captain?"

"So I was saying the old lady sold the business, and there are no records with them, but the lady was insistent that a bill of quantities and amount along with the description of the materials would have been handed over to the customer. So maybe Robert had the bill. See, something like this. She gave me a copy of another bill." He showed a sample bill handed over by the old widow to him.

"Fairly detailed, I must say, very meticulous. She was not lying about his ability to record everything. I will ask Andy to look for it. If it was handed over, it must be at the mansion. Father never threw anything out at all. Everything was recorded. Good thing he is coming over, he can see this bill. He will know exactly what to look for."

"Yeah," agreed the captain. "So now is the main update for you. We ran the scan on three things: the bullet extracted from our deputy last night, who was executed. The bullet recovered from the funeral, which hit Lisa, and the bullet extracted from Robert with the gun found on the killer last night. The gun used is of the same type and manufacture, but I am afraid there are two different guns involved. This is not the murder weapon used to kill Robert. The other two shots were fired from the shooter's gun."

"How can that be? You said it yourself, both were Magnums."

"Yes, I did, but the markings on the bullet fired from his gun last night and the shell do not match the markings on the bullet we extracted from Robert. You have to understand that every gun when it fires a bullet leaves a distinctive marking on the bullet, and we can easily match that with the gun, but this is different. See these three photos: the first is the bullet that was used to shoot Robert, the second and third are the bullets extracted from our deputy last night, and the third is the one from the funeral. Look at them. See the distinct patterns."

Charles examined both photographs.

Charles' phone beeped. It was Darcy's message, "On my way." Charles kept the phone on the side.

"See that, Charles. They are completely distinct, not even remotely the same."

"Why don't we trace the bullet then, the serial number on it, where it was manufactured?"

"Good question. Getting to that now," said the captain. "The shot that was fired at Robert was from his gun, which we have not found yet, so we cannot match the bullet to it, but the gun was registered in his name. We know that for sure, so naturally, the bullet was also issued in his name, and we verified them from the records of the seller. So it is safe to assume it was an authentic and legal purchase, and there is nothing wrong there. We even called the manufacturer, and he has cross-verified the records. But this bullet and the gun—the one that was used to shoot our officer—were illegally sourced. There were no markings or serials on it from which we could trace who had manufactured it, and it does not match any of the bullets available here. It seems like it was illegally obtained from overseas."

"Paulo," said Charles.

"There is a good chance that is the case. We can't be sure of it, but we are on the lookout for Paulo. Even a red corner notice has been issued now. The Interpol has been informed too. He steps one foot in this jurisdiction, and he will be caught. The guy was a trained shooter, there was no doubt about it. The way he shot the officer, it could not have been done by a novice. You are one really lucky guy, Charles, you survived him twice. He could have shot you, but he got surrounded by us, and the way killers are trained, he knew the best chance he had to escape was with a hostage, so he kept you alive for it."

Charles thought quietly for a brief moment, recollecting when he was held hostage, then said, "No wonder he did not kill me even though he could have so easily."

"Yes, because he knew we would have killed him in retaliation. He could not risk that. I remember that night you told me he kept saying something."

"I told you he said 'Audii' something, most likely gibberish, nothing more."

"Often, when nervous and stressed, killers have been seen repeating a certain word or action. Some rub their faces, some swear, and some say words to reassure themselves of survival. Maybe it was that."

"Yeah, it could be that, Captain. Did we find out who he was at least, or is that a mystery too?"

"Yes, his official name was Dominico, popularly known as 'The Silencer', wanted in at least five jurisdictions for murders and homicide. Born in Colombia. We asked one of our Interpol officers to inquire about his family, but there was none. He was an orphan. Best of the kind for Paulo to pick up. Rightly so because he worked for him. We have checked the records. He was seen with Paulo on various occasions, one of his top shooters and bodyguards," the captain said and showed the photos.

"Well, we got the best of the best then, didn't we?"

"We sure did. We got the best. Anything else about last night, Charles?"

"Not that I can think of. My condolences to the family of the deputy."

"We are taking care of that sensitively. If there is nothing else, Lisa and you can give your statements, and when Darcy comes, you know the drill. Her statement is the most important since she fired the shot, and you two can corroborate it."

"That's pretty much it. Darcy messaged a few minutes back, she is on her way, Captain."

Darcy came storming in and panting, "Sorry I am late. I hope I did not make you wait too long."

"No, not long. We were just about to give our statements."

"You haven't given them till now? Any updates for me as well?"

"In summary, everyone still has their cufflinks gifted by father. The gun of the killer is not the one used to kill father, and Cliff was let go from protective custody since the killer is dead. I'll share the details at home. Right now, you have to give your statement, since the shot was... (Charles paused and choked a bit), you know, fired by you to save me."

"I did what was right and you know it."

"Alright, don't start again now. You guys go over to the deputy and give your statements."

Charles and Lisa got up and walked out of his lodge, and Darcy followed them. While they walked, they could faintly hear the radio behind the captain as his door closed.

Chapter 8

The Mishap

The police radio behind the captain went off, "All units, request your attention. There has been an accident. A white car has been found—I repeat, a white car. The driver lost control and drove off the road. No other casualties."

Charles, Darcy, and Lisa were sitting with the deputy, reiterating the incident of the previous night. The captain barged in, "There has been an accident, Charles. I am heading out. If you need anything, you know how to reach me."

"Should I come along?"

"No, you sort this out first. Your life as it is is very eventful nowadays. Must be another drunken ride."

"Thanks, Captain. Will do."

The captain stormed out of the station with a few officers, while the three got their statements recorded. After about an hour, the captain called Charles, "Charles, are you done with the statements?"

"Almost. Lisa is just finishing with hers, then we head home. Do you need something?"

"Well, I am afraid I have some bad news."

"I have had my share of bad news for the day."

"You would want to hear this. It's Andy. He has been in an accident. Come over as soon as you are done."

"What!!!" Charles stood up in astonishment and said, "Andy, but how can that be? The killer was shot dead last night. Who did this?"

"What happened to Andy?" both Lisa and Darcy ask with fear in their voices.

"He has been in an accident. Wait, let me get the facts. I will tell you," Charles continued talking on the phone.

"Is he okay, Captain?"

"I am afraid not. He is hurt badly and unconscious. We have sent him to the hospital. His car drove off the road, rolled over twice, and then landed in the ditch. We have pulled his car out, and it is in bad shape. Come, I'll send you the location. You have to see this."

"You girls finish your statement and come by. Right now, I have to leave urgently. Andy has been in an accident and is grievously hurt. He has been sent to the hospital. I am taking the car. I'll send the location to you both."

Charles stormed out of the station, heading to the crash site.

"Oh God, not Andy too," said Lisa in a quivering voice. "When will all this end?"

"He will be fine," replied Darcy as tears rolled down her cheeks. "He will be fine."

"Let's go to the hospital after this and see him. I am really scared. I don't want to lose him." Darcy nodded in agreement.

After finishing their statements, they ask the deputy if he could find out where Andy was hospitalised. The deputy inquired about it from the concerned officer on the radio and gave them the address. "Hope he recovers, ma'am. I am told the accident was bad."

They both headed to the hospital. They called a taxi and quickly jumped in. "It's an emergency. Please hurry, foot the pedal."

They reached the hospital and asked for Andy.

"Are you family?" asked the receptionist.

"Yes, we are."

She pointed them to the lift: "Third floor on the left. You will see the ICU. When you come back down, I have a few documents that you need to sign."

They both shuddered when they heard the word ICU. They entered the lift, went to the third floor, and turned left to the ICU.

"No one is allowed inside, ma'am," said the guard on duty.

"But we have to go inside. We have a family member there."

"It's intensive care, ma'am. We cannot risk contamination. You can see from that window there."

They both went to the window on the side.

"There," pointed Lisa inside the ICU at Andy.

Andy was seen covered in blood, and a nurse was holding a bandage to his head, trying to stop the bleeding. Just then, another nurse came running with the doctor and pulled the curtain, obscuring the view.

Darcy hugged Lisa.

"He will be okay," Lisa hugged her back, being strong about the situation.

Just then, Lisa got a call from Charles: "Why aren't you girls here yet?"

"We took the cab and came to the hospital instead. We thought it'd be better if we stayed with Andy rather than coming to the crash site. Anyway, we have nothing to do there. You are a better person for the job on that front."

"I guess you are right. This would have been a waste of time. Good decision. I'll see you there later. Lisa… How is he?"

"We only got a glimpse of him before they started their procedures. Not in good shape, Charles. I won't lie."

At the accident scene, Charles was seen with the captain standing on the side while Andy's car was pulled out by cranes. The car had turned over at least twice when it slid off and was completely mangled.

"It's a miracle he survived given the condition his car is in. Did he drink, Charles?"

"No, Andy never had any."

"It did rain last night, the road is still wet. Maybe he skidded off the road. There are skid marks on the road where he went off. See there," the captain pointed.

"Do you think someone tried to kill him, Captain?"

"We can't rule that out, not with all that is happening. But at this moment, it seems like an accident. There was no other car here, no other tyre tracks were found, nothing of that sort. Maybe he took the turn at high speed and skidded off the road."

"It can't be. Andy was always careful and never reckless like this. He drove really slowly."

The car was pulled out, and they slowly lowered it on the side of the road. The car was damaged from all sides. It was examined by the experts on the site and also by Charles and the captain.

"It's damaged from all sides. Even if someone rammed it, there is no way to find out. It's damaged so badly."

"I see that, Captain," he mumbled.

"What are you babbling about now, Charles?" replied the captain in anger.

"I called him, Cap. I called him to the station. I could have met him at home, and none of this would have happened."

"Charles, you really need to go see a psychiatrist or something because this is getting too much for you. Let's go back to the hospital and let the experts handle this. Maybe Andy can shed better light on what happened. We can reach there before he gains his senses."

Charles nodded in agreement. They drove to the hospital. Lisa and Darcy were there outside the ICU.

"How is he?" asked Charles.

"I don't know. They won't tell us anything until he is out of the ICU."

"Wait here. Let me try," said the captain.

He went to the guard outside the ICU, who pointed him further down the hall to a room. The captain went in.

"He was covered in blood, Charles. I am really scared for him."

"He will be fine, Lisa. Don't worry. Let's not say our prayers yet. He will be fine."

Darcy just stood in silence and was depressed. Just then, the captain was seen walking back from the room down the hall.

"Anything, Captain?"

"There were multiple broken bones and a concussion to his head. He is unconscious. If his state does not improve or if he does not regain consciousness, the doctor says (sighs) that it can be assumed that he is in a coma."

"It has to be that bastard Cliff. I told you from the start," said Darcy hysterically. "I told you. You let him go this morning, and look at what he did. I did not say anything in the station."

"How can you blame someone like that, Darcy? We spoke to him, and he cooperated."

"I don't need evidence, Charles. Think about it. He stands to gain the most from his father's being gone. The firm becomes his. He had control over the finances as well. He knew his father made millions. Then where did they all go? It's like all of his money just vanished. He must have known Andy would eventually find something. That's why, the moment he got out, he went after Andy. He knew Andy would come up with some evidence. I know he is lying. Since the day Mr. Grey came and read his father's will, I knew something was off. I saw my father's finances a year ago. He asked me to help with them. There were five million easy transactions in just one of his accounts, and I don't know how many accounts he had. Where did all that money go?"

"You knew all this, and you decided to tell me now? We never considered money a motive, Darcy, not even once."

"Neither did I, Charles, but this baffles me. Where did it all go?"

While this conversation was going on, the captain received a call. "Go for captain. Yes, yes, I get it. Thanks."

"They found a little residue of white paint on Andy's car. They are scanning for more indications. They have further stated that the paint could be old, and they need to do some tests. There was only one set of tyre tracks, so the possibility of another car being there has been ruled out."

"Cliff has a white car. We saw it in the footage," exclaimed Darcy. "Do I need to prove anything more? Please, brother, just trust me this once."

"It won't harm checking on him once. We can say it was for precaution and safety," stated the captain, "but it has to be strictly professional, no accusations. You understand. We find things normal at his house, and we walk out, no questions asked. You hear me? Am I clear to the three of you? Or do I go alone?"

All three nodded in absolute agreement. "Let's go."

"I would like to stay here with Andy, if that is okay with all of you," said Lisa. "This is all too much for me, and I need a break from all this. All this uncertainty is killing me. I cannot focus on so many directions and so many variables at the same time. At least here, I know I am waiting for only one person to get better. Plus, I think I might end up on a bed here too."

"We understand," said Charles, "and we will see you at the mansion."

The three of them walked out of the hospital to check on Cliff.

"You have a good one there, Charles," said the captain.

"I know. I just hope it doesn't get too much for her. I don't want her to leave."

"She won't. She may be scared, but she loves you. Otherwise, she would have been long gone by now."

They stepped out. Charles turned to Darcy and asked, "Why don't you leave your car and come with us? Lisa can drive it back to the mansion."

"Erm, my car?"

"Yes, your car, Darcy."

"My car had an oil leak. I saw it leaking in the driveway last night. So I dropped it at the repair station, then met my friend, then came here."

Charles then remembered that when he walked out in the morning, Darcy's car was parked in the garage, and there was no oil on the floor.

"Me and Lisa saw the driveway. It was sparkling clean in the morning, and your car seemed fine."

"It rained heavily last night," shouted Darcy in anger. "It must have washed off. Keep your detectives in check. Do we need to take separate cars now, or can you keep it under control?"

"Shut up, both of you. Fighting like little kids. The last thing I want is for you two to implode right now. Now get in the car, and let's go. I am tired of playing the disciplinarian here."

Chapter 9

Face to Face With the Killer

They drove towards Cliff's lodge up the mountain.

"Cliff is not going to move back to his mansion anytime soon," he said. "He said the lodge is more peaceful and safer for him. Away from the crowd and clatter," said the captain.

They arrived at the lodge and everything seemed normal. They got down and rang the bell. Cliff answered, "Who is it?"

"It's Nate Cliff, open up. Here for a routine check."

The gate buzzed. "Come on in."

Inside the gate, on the short driveway, they saw his car parked. The car's white colour raised their doubts further.

"See!!!" jumped Darcy.

"Let's check it out before going in," said Charles. "It will only take a minute."

"What did I say about the accusations part? You both don't listen, do you?" said the captain in a stern tone.

"I am not accusing anyone of anything. All I am saying is we can have a quick look before we go in."

Charles opened the car door, and Nate tried to stop him.

"Shit, let's go after him before he files a case of illegal trespass against us."

They got out of the car, went behind Charles, and stopped behind Cliff's car.

"It's okay, see? Can we now go inside, please, Charles?"

"Wait."

"Now what?"

Charles took out his phone and switched on the torch to go to the front of the car inside the garage, "Aa haa, see... see that."

"Now do you agree with me?"

The captain was astonished. The car was damaged from the front and the left light was broken. It seemed okay from the back.

"This is why it was parked half in the garage. He knew we would come to check on him after Andy's accident, and from the back, the car looked perfectly fine. No one would have noticed and he would have gotten it repaired in a few days. At his mansion, servants would have noticed but here it was only him and no one. The perfect place to hide his guilt."

"I have to agree with Charles on this, Captain. It gives us a good reason to search his premises."

"I'll call for backup. You may be right. Let's detain him at least."

"See, I told you. I told you it was him. You never trusted me, brother."

The captain shushed Darcy. "This still isn't enough, Darcy. We can question him, but it's not enough to prove he is guilty. Let's play it smart and see how this plays out. Maybe we can get him to confess if I scare him a bit."

Cliff opened the main door of the lodge. "Hey, you guys coming in for a drink or what?"

The captain responded in a loud, stern voice, holding up his gun. "Cliff Dreker, I have to detain you for further questioning. Put your hands where I can see them."

Cliff responded in a frightened, stammering voice, "What! I have done nothing wrong. You let me go from protective custody this morning, only to arrest me at night. What is happening? I told you I had done nothing."

He walked to the captain with his hands in the air. The backup also arrived.

"We will see, Cliff."

"What are you arresting me for? You know I did not murder Robert. You yourself gave me protective custody."

"You are being arrested for attempting to murder Andy this time, not Robert."

"Andy, your butler," he pointed at Charles, "why would I do that?"

"Where were you during the day?"

"At home, here, where else would I be? You can check with my office. I have been here all day, taking calls. This is bullshit. I want my lawyer here this time. I am done playing your stupid games. I know my rights and my defence. I will mop the floor with your department. So if you have any concrete charges, let's hear them. Otherwise, get off my property."

Charles looked around. "There are no cameras here. How do we know you never left the premises?"

"Really, Charles? After everything I told you truthfully, do you think I have anything to do with this at all? I am a lawyer. I know my rights. You cannot detain me without something. Check the GPS on my phone. It'll show I never left the lodge."

"The phone can be left behind, Uncle Cliff. We just want to ask more questions," Charles responded. "Why is your car damaged from the front?"

"Damaged? I have not moved the thing in days. The driver must have used it. I have no idea why it is damaged. I have just heard this from you."

"Where is Darcy now?" asked the captain.

"Here," said Darcy, standing near the garage. "I thought it'd be best to keep my distance."

"Stay here, Darcy. Let the team search the premises."

"You cannot do anything here without a warrant. Get out of my premises now."

"Well, good thing I brought one," the captain showed him the warrant.

They detained Cliff, put him in the police car, and took him to the police station.

"When did you get the warrant, Captain?"

"I didn't. It's his old warrant to search. I hid the date with my thumb," smiled Nate.

"Finally, finally, they have him. Finally, father can rest in peace now," said Darcy.

The captain patted Darcy on the back. "We still need more proof to put him behind bars. He knows that too. We need cogent proof. Search the area thoroughly, sweep everything. We have him only for a few hours before he gets out and lawyers up. Do your best. Double shifts, no breaks. I want every pebble and every inch checked."

Charles called up Lisa.

"How is he?"

"Same, no change, all bandaged up. What about there?"

"It was him, Lisa. His car was all damaged from the front, and it gives us a good reason to search for him properly now. If we find what we are looking for, it's case closed. I can't believe I trusted him."

"What, Cliff?" said Lisa in astonishment. "Right under our noses, and we never realised. But you said he was innocent, Charles, then?"

"Well, circumstances change, Lisa. He is still saying he had nothing to do with it, but it's hard to believe since the proof is against him. He had something to do with Andy's accident."

"Well, he will get what's coming to him for doing this to Andy."

"I am leaving here for the mansion now. See you there."

"Okay, see you. Bye."

Darcy walked up to Charles. "Let's go home if that is okay with you."

"I still can't believe uncle Cliff would do such a thing. Father gave him everything he ever wanted and practically loved the man."

"Well, killers lie. They believe in their own reality. If they were honest, why would you need detectives, right, Charles?"

"You are right, Darcy. I owe you an apology for not believing in you earlier."

"It's okay. We were all under a lot of pressure. We were attacked from all sides. A little bit of hysteria is given."

A voice from the back called, "Captain, over here."

The captain walked to the deputy, pointing to something on the side of the garage near the bushes. "There, see that. Something is reflecting the light."

The captain asked for another torch to see clearly. He then reached in to grab it. He was astonished at what he found. He turned around to Charles.

Charles, seeing this, asked the captain, "Is that the..."

"We got him, Charles. We got the lying, cheating bastard."

The captain brought it to him and showed him the single cufflink on the floor. "We got him."

Charles saw the cufflink in astonishment, and it quickly turned into anger. "I'll kill him. I'll kill him with my own bare hands now."

"Relax, Charles. Let the law take its course now. We have enough to put him away for a long time."

"Father gave him everything, and this is how he repays him," Charles responded, infuriated.

"I have also sent a team over to check his mansion. I will send this cufflink to the forensics. If it's silver, we have him."

They all waited at the lodge while the team searched the area. After two hours, the captain said, "I don't think there is anything else here. Let's meet tomorrow at the station and take it from there." They all got into the car and drove home.

"Finally, finally, we have him, Charles, the killer of our father. This time, there are no dead ends and no closed loops. He must have hired that hitman to do his dirty work for him."

Charles kept quiet. He was just extremely angry. The killer was right in front of him the whole time, right there, and he let him go. He didn't do anything about it. They reached the mansion.

"Not the same without Andy," said Lisa as she opened the door, "but still home."

Charles received a call from the hospital.

"Yes, yes, okay, I understand," he spoke into the phone.

"What happened?" asked Darcy.

"He is stable but, at the moment, unconscious. Doctors are saying it's confirmed he is in a coma. They will observe him for a few days and then make a decision. It could be that he revives."

"Still, we had a great achievement today," Lisa agreed. Charles just nodded and kept quiet.

"Dinner?" asked Darcy.

"I don't feel like having anything. I am still riled up about Andy and all that happened today," Lisa said.

"I am worried about him too. I don't feel like having anything either. Let's go and sleep. Hopefully, now things will be calm in our lives," Charles replied.

Lisa and Charles nodded in agreement. Darcy went up to her room and shut the door. Lisa started climbing the stairs. "Are you coming, hon'?"

"No, I'll be there in some time. I just need some alone time if you don't mind."

“Not at all. Take your time. Come when you feel okay.”

Charles sat down in the armchair and breathed a sigh of relief. “Finally, things are over, father. Finally, we can rest and take it easy. But I wish I had caught him before. Andy would have been here with us right now.”

Chapter 10

The Money Trail

Charles leaned back further in the chair and thought, "We have him. Then why does it feel like something's amiss? Maybe it's just in my head. Maybe I wanted it to be someone else with all the mystery going around. But what about the millions father had? Where did it go? Darcy also corroborated it."

Charles decided to put this theory to the test. He called up Norma, "Hi Norma, sorry to bother you so late."

"Hi, Charles. This better be important. It's a late hour."

"Yes, it is. It could not wait until morning. It relates to father and his finances. Since you had access to some, I thought I would ask you on the phone rather than troubling you to come to the station tomorrow."

"Well, I did not have access to everything, but to some, yes. I hope I can be of help."

"Norma, do you remember, just as an idea, how much money my father had a few months before his demise, before he, you know, stopped coming to the office?"

"Well, that's a weird and vague question to ask Charles. Like I said, I did not have access to everything."

"Do you remember anything at all? We are also trying to investigate a money-syphoning angle as well. The money in the firm accounts, maybe?"

"Can I state something off the record? If it's worthwhile, you can always get a warrant and check it out. A few months ago, he did ask me to get his account statement from one of the banks. I happened to sneak a peek before they put the statement in the envelope and sealed it for Robert."

"So, what did you see?"

"I saw the total was about seven million something."

"Seven, you say," said Charles in astonishment.

"Yup, seven it was—seven big ones. But it didn't come as a surprise, given the money he made for the firm. I didn't want to share this because it does not look professional on my part. But given the circumstances, any information could be helpful. But what relevance does this hold?"

Charles decided to keep the details to a minimum. "Well, like I said, we are still investigating. We need to see all possible angles. I will let you know if anything develops further in this regard."

"All right, love, good night then," Norma said, and she hung up the phone.

Andy was right, thought Charles. Seven million, according to Norma, but he left us only one million in his account. Something does not add up. Where did all that money go?

Did Cliff take the money and then kill him? But we saw him leave on camera. The hard drive was missing too. We don't know for sure because we didn't see the shooter. Maybe he left, then came back from the side. The door was made for the clients to come and go without going into the house. He came back and then shot him, removed the hard drive, and went off. What about the gun? Where did he hide that? So many questions, so many thoughts, Charles mused.

"I need to speak with him to find out for sure what actually happened. Hopefully, this time he will tell me the truth," Charles thought, contemplating all possible scenarios of how Cliff could have done it and gotten away with it.

"Maybe I am overthinking this. Maybe Darcy is right. Maybe I should concentrate now on where the money went and check it with the bank tomorrow," Charles decided, making one final call to the captain.

"Yeah, Charles?"

"Sorry to trouble you, Captain, but I need a warrant to check the past financials of my father with his bank. There is some money missing, and I would like to investigate that aspect."

"Sure thing, come and take it in the morning from the station. We could find out more about what happened. Maybe that clarifies things more."

The next morning, Charles went to the station to meet the captain.

"Here is what you need, Charles. And there is some further good news. The cufflink we bagged last night is made of silver. Now we have proof beyond doubt that he did it. We have him for sure now. He left this morning with his lawyer. We have a date for court now."

Charles smiled and said, "Well, that takes care of everything. Father can finally be peaceful now."

"One last thing, Charles. A team of officers also went to Cliff's mansion in the city and searched it thoroughly, but they did not find the murder weapon. That is still missing. No one knows where it went. Had we found it, the case would have been airtight."

"It's alright, Captain. At least we got him. That's what matters to me."

Charles took the papers and headed to the bank. There, he met the manager and explained the entire thing. The manager saw the warrant and said, "A few days ago, one Mr. Cliff Dreker also came for the past records. We refused to hand them over to him since he was neither of the joint signatories authorised by the late Robert Knight. He kept emphasising that he was his partner at the firm, and he would have to do it legally if we did not help out. He even threatened to defame us and bury us deep in litigation. We explained to him again and again that we needed both the signatures of the joint owners to access the accounts. We are at the same impasse here." He then paused for a moment and said, "However, since you have a warrant and are also here in the capacity of a detective investigating a crime, we will provide the information you require. I still don't understand why you all can't just work this out amongst yourselves and submit a simple joint application."

He signalled the accountant in the bank and gave him the warrant, whispering in his ear. After a few minutes, the accountant came back and handed over the entire statement of Robert's account. Charles sat there and examined it for over an hour. He noticed that Robert did earn millions, but since the past year, the money had either been withdrawn in "cash" or transferred to some account.

He called for the manager again and asked for his help to explain. He examined the statements.

"Well, you see, here these transactions state the money was withdrawn in cash from other branches of ours, and these are transferred to different accounts, maybe payments for some service."

"Alright, and what about these ones where the millions are transferred at a time?"

"I thought you would pick up on those. We also inquired about this from Mr. Robert, since we are required under law to inform the clients of any irregular transactions. To which he simply stated, 'It's my other bank overseas, and all taxes are paid on the income along with the transaction, so nothing to worry about there.'"

"That's it? Did you not ask for any further explanation?"

"No, you see, Robert was one of our, how can I put it, very elite clients. People, we do not push much because we need their accounts in our banks. We do not trouble them unless it's a case of financial fraud. In this case, there is no law stopping anyone from transferring their own money into their accounts. That was a good enough explanation for us."

"The other bank? What does that mean?"

"Means another bank. What is the confusion in this?"

"How do you know it was a bank?"

"All banks have codes. See next to the transaction this number. If it's cash, it says withdrawn in cash for self." He showed another transaction in the account, "All banks have codes.

"Can you tell me which one this is and its location?"

"Well, that is the reason why we called Mr. Robert. This bank does not reflect in our systems if you understand what I am trying to tell you."

"No, I don't. Can you be more clear?"

"I cannot, but since you are his son, I am giving you more already. You have to be smart to pick up the hints now. Read between the lines. The bank could be, let's say, somewhere on some island outside our jurisdiction. Think about it."

"Paulo," thought Charles.

The manager got up and said, "Good day to you, sir. Oh, and before you ask, I believe the next obvious question would be if it can be recovered. The answer is that it cannot be recovered because we don't know which bank it has gone to or where. These banks normally use dummy accounts."

Charles was even more confused now. First, his father gets murdered. Now the money goes missing, that too was done by his own father in his knowledge and wisdom. Cliff had also come to the bank, the manager said, maybe to inquire about the same thing. Andy also said he must have had more the day Mr. Grey read the will.

So now, this is another mystery I have to solve. Where did the money go? Or the better question would be, where did father transfer the money and why? Maybe he knew he was in danger, and this was the only way, or maybe he was into something illegal and transferred out the money, so as not to get caught? What did you get yourself into, father?

Charles stepped out of the bank and went to his car, deep in his thoughts. He decided to go home and take time to grasp and accept all that had happened. He was trying to make sense of all that his father did and got into with his clients. Maybe that's how he made so much money—by illegal means, he thought to himself. Maybe he was not a clean man after all.

Charles reached home. Darcy was standing in the driveway, on the side of the garage. Charles parked the car and got out.

"Lovely day, isn't it, Charles? Where did you go off in the morning?"

"Well, I went to our father's bank, and you were right there also, sis. Maybe you are a better detective than me."

"What do you mean?"

"Cliff went to the bank, the manager told me. He wanted the statement of accounts and threatened them with legal action if they did not comply."

"I knew he had something to do with all this. I always had my eyes on him. That does give him a strong, probable cause to murder our father. Money can make you do evil things."

"Father did have loads of money, but for some reason, he himself transferred it to an untraceable account and withdrew the rest. The manager had asked him about these transactions, but his father explained to him that they were authentic. Other than that, he roughly maintained one million in his account and kept withdrawing or transferring the rest. I really don't know what got into our father."

"So you're telling me the money is gone and we can't do anything to get it back."

"Nope, nothing. We could do something if we knew where it went."

"Well, that's a big bummer now, isn't it?" Darcy said in a sad tone, looking down at the driveway.

"Darcy, I thought you would be more upset."

"I am, Charles, but what's gone is gone. I can't help it. I was astonished too when Mr. Grey read the will because I had seen his financials before. He had more money. Before I could say anything, Andy took the words right out of my mouth. The only hope I am clinging to now is if Cliff discloses something in questioning that tells us where it all went."

"I know, but it's rather strange how the money has vanished completely. Maybe Cliff managed something with the bank manager."

"Well, at least one thing is done. We have the killer in custody, and I hope he gets what he deserves."

"Well, they still don't have the murder weapon. I hope they have enough otherwise to convict him."

"Let's just try to live on and move on and see what happens," said Darcy as she walked into the house.

Charles stood at the driveway for a while, looking at the clear blue sky, feeling a bit calm and at ease, trying to grasp and think of the events that happened in the past few days and how they changed his life. He had no parents to fall back on now, no security, and no cushion in case of an emergency. He was on his own now, just him and Darcy. The thought troubled him a bit, but that was the reality now. He would have to move into the mansion now to take care of it with Darcy and Andy. He had to be the grown-up in the house now.

"Andy," he remembered. Charles took out his phone and called the hospital.

"Yes, yes, are you a family member?" said the voice on the phone.

"Yes, I am. Is there any update on his health?"

"Well, not much. He is the same. Still sleeping. No movement yet, but the doctors are happy he is stable now."

"Thank you for that. I will come by during the day to check on him and talk to the doctor." Charles kept the phone down and walked to the house.

Inside, he saw Lisa sitting. "Hey, how are you feeling? Where did you run off to?"

"Better," said Charles, "I went to the bank for some work. They want me down at the station during the day when they talk to Cliff. I don't think I can face him even after what he has done. I trusted him. My father trusted him as a brother. I gave him everything."

"Well, at least you have him. He won't be able to harm any more people now."

"I don't know, Lisa."

"You don't know? What is there not to know?"

"Something doesn't feel right."

"What doesn't feel right?"

"I don't know. I can't seem to get that feeling of closure, you know when it's over."

"I think you are just overworked and overtired with all that has unfolded in the past few weeks. You need rest and a nice vacation with someone you love," smiled Lisa, pointing to herself.

"Yeah, Darcy and I could use a vacation," said Charles amusingly.

"How mean!!" replied Lisa, smiling. "Well, I think you should go to your room and rest. Take the day off. I have to go for some work. I'll swing by and check on Andy on the way back. Just get some rest today. Everyone needs a break."

"Well, I called the hospital. Andy is the same, just slightly more stable."

"Still, he is family, and we should be there for him. You rest, I'll handle this. It's the least I can do." She gave Charles a kiss and left for the day.

Chapter 11

The Secret Compartment

Charles sank deep in his chair, looked at the ceiling and thought, "Something else has to be there, especially the money." Charles then got up and started climbing the stairs to his room, still in deep thought. He went inside the room and sat on the floor, at the side of the bed.

"Cliff was out, we saw him leave. When did he come back? How did he manage to do it? There are cameras all over the place. Maybe he found a blind spot? If we had the footage of the camera in the study, things would have been so easy."

While sitting there and staring at the room, deep in his thoughts, he happened to glance at his desk, where he spent his entire childhood studying. They were two of a kind, this one and the father's desk in the study, the same in design, just a bit smaller than the one in the study. Charles went closer to the desk and sat on the chair. "I wish you were here, father. I really need your guidance."

Charles then started to look at the things on the desk and in the drawers. Suddenly, his attention went to the side of the desk, where the secret compartment was. The hollow cavity under the drawer, where he had hidden lots of things in the past. This was the one place he and Andy knew about.

Andy used to leave notes for Charles about things he did not want Robert to find out, like the hidden chocolate cake he kept for him. Charles put his hand inside and found something there. He found a book and two papers folded inside the cover of it. It was the book his father left Andy.

"Why are these things here?" he thought to himself. He realised that Andy must have kept them here for him. Maybe this is what Andy was talking about on the phone when he wanted to come and meet urgently.

Charles kept the book aside and opened the first folded paper. Yellow in colour, it looked as if it were a few years old. It was the bill for the cufflinks. Charles noticed nothing peculiar and kept it on the desk. The total number of pairs added up. The captain was right about this. "I knew if there was anyone who could find it, it was Andy."

He then saw the other paper kept for him, fairly white. This seemed recent. It was a bill for a camera installed last year.

"That's weird," he thought to himself. "Bill for one camera. There are already so many in the mansion. Why add more? Maybe one camera was repaired." But then he noticed in the bill that an amount for installation was charged. "Why would installation be charged again for a camera repair?"

He took out his phone and searched for the model of the camera. The camera was not like the traditional wired ones already installed in the mansion.

"But where was this even installed? It's a huge mansion. How would I know where it was?"

He thought why not start where everything happened at the study? Andy had also mentioned father-enhancing security due to the nature of his clients in the study.

He went downstairs into the study and started looking around. He started from the desk and then walked around. He did not find anything there. The desk had huge bookshelves around it. He thought where could it be?

He started looking around but saw nothing standing where he was, except the old camera, which was missing its footage, and the camera outside, which recorded the shooting. He then thought to himself that the killer must have followed the wires to reach the DVR. He also started looking for the wires, looking around and the corners of the wall to find them. He saw the white wires of the old cameras going into the wall. He then looked at the floor to see where they came out behind the shelf. They were not there.

While stepping back, his shoe got stuck in something. Charles tripped and fell to the floor. "Crap," he said. He turned around to see that it was the carpet. It was a bit loose there. He lifted it and saw a little black wire going under it. He pulled it a little and then kept following it. The wire went behind the bookshelf, the one behind the father's desk.

Charles tried to squeeze in, following the wire with one hand. It came up and went inside a book. Charles pushed the book out a bit and then stepped out from behind the bookshelf. He came to the front and pulled the book. It was a fake one. He opened it and smiled.

There was a camera inside. This is what Andy must have found out. He looked inside. It was an independent wireless camera, alright, with just one black wire for the power supply. He was so happy to see this camera because it would have recorded the face of the killer and everything that happened.

His happiness all of a sudden turned into anger. "No, no, no," he exclaimed, infuriated. The memory card was missing. It wasn't there. Charles checked the bookcam three to four times but did not find it.

"Maybe this is what Andy was trying to tell me on the phone. Maybe it fell here only."

He kept the book back and started looking for the memory card—a tiny little thing that would be difficult to find. He looked around the shelf but could not find it.

Charles decided to keep this to himself and not share it with anyone until he found out what was on the memory card and how it was linked to Andy and his father. First, he had to find that little thing.

He ran out, quickly got into his car, and drove off. He reached the hospital where Andy was and went into his room. Andy was on the bed, lying still, with a drip in his arm and a mask on his face. Charles paused for a moment, seeing him like this. He sat next to him, held his hand, and thought, "You wanted to tell me, you did. And I didn't realise how important it was." Staring at Andy in that condition, he promised, "I will find out soon what it was that you wanted to tell me."

Charles then went to the wardrobe and opened it. Andy's clothes were there, covered in blood. Charles felt sad but went through their pockets. His wallet was there, as was his phone, but the memory card wasn't there.

He then remembered that his car had toppled twice. Maybe it fell out of his pocket and into the car. Charles rushed out of the hospital and drove to the police impound, where the car was kept in its damaged condition.

Charles did not know if he would find anything important, but he had a strong hunch. This could end it all, give him the closure he wanted, and give him the peace he desired. He reached the impound, signed in, flashed his badge, and asked the in-charge to take him to the vehicle.

They took him to the vehicle. It was damaged all across. "Are the forensics done with the vehicle?" Charles asked.

"Yes, they are."

"Can you get me a copy of the report?"

Charles tried to open the door, but it was stuck.

"Help me open this door," he requested.

"The door will not open like this. Wait, let me get the equipment for it and also a copy of your report."

The mechanic came back with a copy of the report and handed it over. Under the heading of items found, there was no memory card listed.

The mechanic towed the car to a hydraulic hook to pull the door. They pulled the door out. "There," said the mechanic. Charles quickly pushed him aside and started looking for the memory card inside the vehicle.

"Something particular are you looking for?" asked the mechanic.

"Just checking the whole thing to see if something got missed," said Charles.

"Let me know if you need anything," the mechanic said, going back to what he was doing.

Charles continued to search the vehicle for the memory card. The tiny little thing could have gone anywhere. He looked everywhere in the car: the glove compartment, the floor, under the mats, under the seat, every corner, and every cavity. He even ripped out the carpet, but could not find it. He then walked to the front of the car and opened it, finding nothing unusual. He still checked a few areas and corners. He then went behind the car and opened the trunk, but it was not there.

The same feeling of failure crept in again. Charles got frustrated and yelled. The mechanics at the workshop looked at him from a distance, paused for a second, then got back to work.

Maybe Cliff took it, he thought. He glanced at the spare tyre and took a photo of it just in case. Still, he had nothing.

Charles slammed the open trunk of the car in anger. It closed, but it reflected something. Charles got interested and took a closer look. It wasn't the card, but something else. He saw scraped lines of white paint on the trunk. He immediately took a picture and took some of it off in an evidence bag. It could prove the killer was there.

Charles then called up the station. "I need an analysis done. Send someone to my house. I'll explain when they reach."

Charles then got into his car and drove up to Cliff's lodge. His car was there. He went near the car, looked for something, and again scraped a bit of paint from an evidence bag.

Charles then drove back to the spot of Andy's accident. He didn't know what he was looking for, but he knew both the accident and the murder were somehow connected. He started looking at everything carefully again.

He looked around. The skid marks were still there but faded. There was one set of tracks. He sat down on the road and started examining it. He saw something on the road, took out his pocket knife, scraped out a piece, and put it in an evidence bag again. Charles was confident about something now. He then measured the tyre skid marks and went back home.

At the mansion, Charles went to where Andy's car used to be parked and looked around the driveway. He bent down for a closer look and spotted something, then picked up a few stones and bagged them. He then went around the garage. Darcy's and Lisa's cars were parked there. He opened both cars and looked around, then sat in both for a while doing something.

Charles then stepped out of the garage and, while walking to the mansion, noticed a few pieces of paper in the trash can on the side of the garage. He thought to himself, "This bin is rarely used," and picked up the pieces, taking them into the mansion. After half an hour, he came running out of the mansion, got into his car, and drove off.

Charles then called the captain.

"Yes, Charles?"

"Captain, I need a search party."

"What the hell is going on, Charles? First a forensic team, now a search party?"

"Just trust me. Send them to this location. I am sending the location to you."

Charles went about the day and returned home in the evening. In his room, he watched the video of his father being shot again and again, looking for things he may have missed. To his astonishment, he realised something, playing the video back and forth repeatedly.

He then finally went down to the dining area with a sense of calm on his face. He had a bag with a shirt containing his father's cufflinks. Lisa was in the dining area having tea. "I told you to rest, Charles, but do you even listen?"

"I had some things to do at the station."

"You went to the hospital also, the nurse told me. Don't you trust me when I say I'll go see Andy? Are you lying to me about something, Charles?"

"No, absolutely not. I had to see him once myself. I was crossing the hospital, so I decided to stop by. Will you help me with something, Lisa?"

"Yeah, sure?"

"Pull on these cufflinks as hard as you can."

"These? Are you recreating the crime scene?"

"Just pull on them really hard. Try to rip them out."

Charles wore the shirt and asked her to pull it, recreating what had happened. Lisa pulled on the sleeves really hard. One cufflink ripped the cuff a bit, but the other broke in the process.

"Well, that did not go as planned," said Lisa, catching her breath. "What are you trying to find out?"

"Nothing seems conclusive to me."

"You are hiding something. I can feel it, Charles. You just ruined your father's cufflinks for no reason."

Charles, at that moment, did not feel like sharing anything, so he decided to lie to her. "No, nothing at all. As you saw, one ripped the shirt, and the other one broke, so I cannot conclude anything. Listen, let this be. It was a stupid test. I want to talk to you about something else that is even more important. I wanted to plan a party for everyone, just as a token of thanks for being with us through all this."

"Really," smiled Lisa, "Why didn't you start with that rather than your dumb experiments?"

"I wanted it to be a surprise. But you know how bad I am at all this. I would have asked you anyway."

Charles gave Lisa the names of the people to be called—a fairly small list. "Invite them, please, while I have a word with the captain." He then kept the shirt and cuffs in his bag and set them aside.

Darcy stepped out of her room. "What's with all the ruckus?"

Charles and Lisa looked up.

"We are having a party, yay!" jumped Lisa. Darcy responded equally ecstatically.

Charles, on the phone, said, "Yes, Captain, the day after, everyone... Did you look okay? Ok. See you the day after then."

"So many things to plan. How could you have done this alone, Charles?" asked Darcy.

"Well, I wanted a simple dinner. I would have eventually asked for your help. If I had told you before, you would have made it grand as always."

Both girls were happy and joyful about planning the event.

The next morning, Charles received a call from the captain. He picked up the phone, listened, smiled, and then hung up. They all prepared for the dinner to be hosted the next evening. Charles kept things calm for the day and finally relaxed in his room.

Chapter 12

The Concealed Reality

The evening finally arrived, and a grand dinner was arranged by the knights for the guests. Everyone important to Robert attended the dinner, including guests from the police department, the firm, Lisa with her family, and a few other near and dear ones. Smiles were abundant, and the atmosphere was filled with joy and acceptance of Robert's passing. Wine glasses kept coming up in the air.

"Toast to Robert!"

There was a sense of peace in everyone's heart.

Charles, Darcy, the captain, and one of his deputies were sitting at the table, casually talking. Lisa was with her family, having a jovial time at the other end of the table.

"Good dinner, Charles. I haven't had so much fun in such a long time," said Nate.

"All for our father. He deserved one last dinner with everyone he loved," Charles replied.

"I hope it brings him peace and rest wherever he is. I miss him," Darcy said calmly.

"If I had to bet, it's heaven, given the number of people he has helped in his lifetime," Charles said.

"So, are you ready for what we talked about, Charles?" asked Nate, his tone filled with concern.

"Yes, I guess it's time," Charles replied.

"Do you want to do this in front of everyone?" Nate asked.

"Let's wait until everyone leaves then. You know who to let out. We will keep it within the family. But be careful. No one should get a hint of what is happening," Charles instructed.

Charles climbed up the stairs to get a better view of the gathering. He took a glass in hand and a spoon for a toast.

"May I have your attention, please?" Charles tapped the glass with the spoon to get everyone's attention.

"Please, everyone, I have a small toast to make. A few words for the departed."

While Charles spoke and the crowd turned to listen, the captain asked two of his deputies to stand at the two exit points, giving them specific instructions about the gathering. People noticed and started murmuring.

"Don't worry, that's just for our safety. We don't want any more surprises. We've had our share for the past few weeks if you know what I mean," the captain reassured, eliciting a restrained sound of laughter from the crowd.

Charles continues in a loud voice, "I am glad you all came. I am thankful and grateful. Father would have loved this had he been here with us. He helped everyone in need and cared for everyone under his wing. With him, you felt like you could conquer the world and be undefeated in front of any adversary. That was my father's personality. Friend to the rich and poor alike. He loved his traditional ways and always gave priority to family. I wish we had spent more time together rather than running in this race of life. That is all he wanted in return: family time—more and more of it. He craved it. When we got busy, he found love with his extended family, all of whom are present here. Always loved and always wanted, the man was omnipresent for everyone, good or bad. Finally, his big one: A client is a client."

Everyone said along with him.

"And I am not the one to judge him."

They laugh a little, then stop.

"As a final goodbye to him, I would request that you all raise your glasses and think of how he changed your life and how he helped you by being in yours."

There was a moment of silence.

"Here is to Robert Knight, best father, great lawyer, loving mentor, and immaculate personality."

"To Robert!" There was a big roar in the room as everyone raised their glass. Some with a smile, some with tears, but all with contentment and closure.

The dinner was over, and everyone left, except Charles, Lisa, Darcy, and the captain with his deputies. Charles and the captain were on one side of the table, while Lisa and Darcy were on the other.

"I wish Andy was here to see all this. He would have loved to see everyone here," said Lisa. Darcy nodded in agreement, folding her hands.

"Now, Captain," whispered Charles with a sigh. "I never thought this would be so difficult, and I will have to be the one to do it."

"What has to be done has to be done. If not you, then me."

The captain got up and signalled the deputies. They both came and stood next to Lisa.

"What is happening, Charles?"

Just then, the door opened, and Cliff entered the room.

"What the hell is he doing here?" Darcy got up in anger and shouted at Charles. Lisa got up, looking really confused and angry.

"We had the wrong person all along. Cliff deserves an apology. Captain, will you?"

"I think they need to hear the truth first, don't they? Innocent until proven guilty, Charles."

"Have you gone mad, Charles, letting this killer into the house after all that he has done? He has caused enough damage as it is. You want him to kill someone in this room again?"

"Please sit down, Lisa, and hear me out. I know what I am doing."

Cliff quietly sat on the opposite side of the table. Both ladies gazed at him with anger.

"He makes a move, and I swear I will kill him myself for what he has done," said Lisa.

Cliff raised both his hands as if to gesture an agreement and chose to keep silent.

Charles stood up and took a few steps back. "Time to jog our memories."

"It all started on the day father was shot. Something has always been missing since the first day, and since that moment, something has not been right. We could not find the gun, nor could we find the killer. We were overlooking one aspect from the start. Something concealed right before our eyes."

"We did. He is right there," Lisa pointed to Cliff.

Charles did not react to Lisa's statement but also politely asked her to hear him out.

"We never found the gun and the killer, so the question that came to my mind was, what was missing from the beginning? What if the killer never left? What if the killer was here all along, and we never realised it? Someone who had access to the mansion and all its areas?"

"Okay, let's go along with this theory of yours. But for the record, you have gone completely mad, Charles," said Darcy. "I told you to keep the detective out."

"Well, I did keep it out. That's why it took so long to realise the reality, believe me. But…anyway. My first suspicion was, what if the killer never got out? What if that person kept hiding? The killer may have left later or the next day, when everything was calm again. So as not to be seen. My second indication was when the deputy told me the hard drive was taken out. I saw the wires the other day and realised they went into the wall. No person who didn't have an idea of the mansion could have reached the DVR to take out the hard drive unless they had x-ray vision and could look through the walls or the floor. The killer had to know where it was and the specific one out of the two. This made me sure the killer was a person who knew the mansion or maybe had access to its blueprints."

"We were all here, Charles. Someone would have seen the killer hiding in the mansion," said Lisa in a worrying tone. "I am not liking where you are going with this. I want to leave now."

Lisa walked to the door, only to be stopped by the deputy. "What is this, Charles? Are we under house arrest now?"

"All will be revealed, have patience."

Lisa was made to sit at the table again.

"See the screen."

Charles played the video of Robert getting shot for everyone in the room to see and paused it when he came back to his desk to type.

"We have all seen this, Charles, and as insensitive as you are, this is really traumatising for me and Darcy to see again and again. I had to go talk to a shrink to get me out of this trauma of being shot. It may be just work for you. For us normal people, it's a huge deal."

Darcy aggressively agreed with Lisa.

Charles ignored them and continued.

"Then the third indication was from father himself. When my father was shot, he went back to the table and to his computer and was typing something on an email addressed to me. A person who is about to die decides to write an email in his final moments rather than to escape. This is never heard of unless the victim knew he had no way to escape or had lost all hope and did not want to escape. The email was minimised and with the letters "FA," which is again very suspicious because in the playback video the deputy showed us, he was seen just typing, which of course is not clear, but he never minimised the window."

"Initials of the killer, like we discussed. We have already taken that into account," said Darcy a bit hesitantly.

"Yes, but then, if you go by that logic, it does not match Cliff's initials or the initials of Paulo. So that means we have the wrong guy, or we never got to the right person. It could only mean that there had to be something else—something he wanted to tell me, something I would pick up, some indication that made him accept his death so easily. I was not sure of what was happening, but things were coming together piece by piece, and then came the fourth indication that made all the sense in the world. The picture became clearer. It was the cufflink on the floor. When the deputy showed me the footage of the camera outside the study, I failed to notice a fairly small yet damaging detail. I realised my glaring mistake when I saw the footage again and again yesterday. I noticed something very, very peculiar. Father had ripped the cufflink out of the killer's shirt. But later, we found the cufflink was on the floor of the study under the table."

"Yes, and it had no prints on it," said Lisa.

"That is the catch, Lisa. Father never dropped it. See the video again."

He played the video again. They all realised that the cufflink was never dropped by Robert.

"The term you are all looking for is called 'Rigour mortis', the stiffening of muscles after a person dies. When his father was shot, he kept his fist closed, and if you see the video, it was still closed when he was on the table. See there," he paused the video.

"So the cufflink should have been still in his fist. Then comes the question: were there two sets of different cufflinks? One in father's hand and one on the floor. When the post-mortem was done later, the cufflink was not found in his hand. The doctor conducting it mistook the pressure mark as a mark of his nail pushed into his skin because his fist was closed at the time of death. The only cufflink was the one on the floor where he was shot, and like you said, Lisa, it was wiped clean. But his hand had a pressure mark on it, according to the post-mortem, which was taken as nothing. So if the cufflink was in his hand, it had to have fingerprints, father's prints, shirt fibres from being ripped out, or the killer's prints. But it was completely clean. So the only logical explanation would be that it was replaced by someone after he was shot. But how could the killer have done that without getting noticed by everyone in the room? The answer lies in the basic art of any magic trick: a slight slip of the hand and quick movement."

Tears started rolling down Charles' eyes. He knew the moment was here. He turned around. "Am I right, Darcy?"

"What?" gasped Darcy as she slipped out of the trance she was in, hearing Charle's narration. "What the hell is wrong with you, Charles? Why are you asking me this?"

Charles wiped his tears and continued.

"Because, Darcy, you were the only one who grabbed father's hand after he passed away on the desk, and the deputy caught you. He didn't know at that time the cufflink was in our father's hand, but you knew. So you jumped to him crying, trying to hold him one last time, and quickly took the cufflink out of his hand.

"You psychopath, if I had done that, wouldn't there be prints of my fingers on the dropped cufflink?" shouted Darcy at the top of her voice.

"When the deputy tried to pull you back, you turned around quickly and dropped the clean cufflink under the table. There were no marks on it because you had kept it conveniently wrapped in your handkerchief. We all saw you wipe your tears with it. Then you placed the real one in your pocket. You knew once the body was taken, they would find the real cufflink in his hand with your prints all over it. So, you decided to play the only card in the book no one would realise—the love of a daughter for her father."

"I need air. My own brother has gone mad," she said and walked to the door, but the deputies stopped her from leaving the room.

"This is madness, Charles. You are taking things too far," Darcy shouted, getting aggressive.

"I could have done this in front of everyone, Darcy. I chose not to. I chose to do this in private. Have the decency to sit, even if you still want to disagree with me. No one is arresting you until I prove it beyond every doubt."

"You have no evidence to prove, I..." Darcy pointed at herself and said, "You executed it the way you are narrating. It's all a theory. Next, you will blame me for Andy's accident as well. This is the last time I see you. After tonight, you are dead to me."

"But how have you come to this conclusion, Charles?" asked Lisa. "Because if it is a hunch, I swear I am walking out with Darcy right now and never coming back. We are so done. I agree with her that you have gone mad and are taking this too far. It could have been Andy. He was in the mansion as well, and all this could have been done by him."

"Okay, you do that if you feel I am wrong. Just hear me out. You have your rights, and no one is stopping you from using them. Now, the question comes: why would Darcy do this?

Well, to answer that, I had to look into her. I looked into her life, her finances, and her business. She was doing really badly and needed loans to keep running the business. No bank would sanction a loan for her since she was already in a lot of debt. So, she turned to the only person who had huge sums of money and who would not ask many questions: Paulo. You went to Paulo for help because he was one of your father's clients. You knew he would be obliged, given the help he got from our father on different occasions. The money was due to Paulo, and when she could not pay it back, he started blackmailing her. You asked father for the money, and he refused since he had already given you so much, hence all the cash withdrawn from his bank accounts. That is why you knew about his finances, even though you admit that he showed the statement to you just once. Being a good and helpful father, he must have realised that Paulo would try to shake you down if you didn't pay up. He called Paulo for a meeting without telling you and must have convinced him that the money would be repaid and that he would leave Darcy alone. Paulo agreed to this proposition and left the country, for reasons best known to him.

But you could not hear all this since father had made the walls soundproof for the study. He knew you were always listening to and watching him. From his loud tone and whatever little you could hear, you assumed the worst. You thought Paulo had come for you to take his money back with interest. Torture and recover, that was Paulo's modus operandi. You thought Paulo came to threaten father, and he would have you killed. The only way to pay him back was through father. Only he had that kind of money. That is why you were so sure about it when Mr. Grey came, but Andy jumped the gun. That is why, after the meeting, Paulo never came back and was never found. It was because he was assured by his father that he would be paid back or compensated for his money. Father kept this from you because he wanted you to spend money more cautiously and understand its value rather than just throwing it into your loss-making business. No matter how much he gave you, you lost it. He wanted you to be under pressure so that you could find other ways to earn it back.

But you thought otherwise, and you confronted him. He refused to give you more money. This is where things got heated, as we saw in the video. He lost his temper. Darcy then pointed the gun at him. You then see father getting calm, trying to ask Darcy to lower the weapon."

Charles played the video further.

"He still did not disclose that the debt was already settled. He then tried to grab the gun, and we all saw what happened. This is why he did not make a run for it or try to save himself. He was shot by one of his own. He walked to his desk and calmly let life leave his body. He had lost everything, even the will to live."

"This is ridiculous, Charles. Nothing makes sense. You are just blabbing things and making them up. Now, can I leave?" said Darcy, banging her hands on the table.

"Indulge my blabbing a little longer. It will all make sense. You were also in shock when he got shot. Accidental or deliberate, it had happened. When you came out of the trance and realised what happened, you decided to act fast because Andy was in the other room, and he must have heard the shot too. Even if the sound was muffled, it was loud enough to raise suspicion. Andy would not come in without being called, but he would if he thought Master Robert was not okay. He would definitely come to check after a reasonable amount of time had elapsed. So, you had to act quickly. Every second was precious. You first decided to get rid of the main piece of evidence, the camera footage. Before going there, you noticed that our father had written something on the computer. That is where the breadcrumbs started. You went to the computer and carefully read what he wrote. You knew you could not touch anything directly with your hands.

It took me a while, but I figured it out. Father had written the word "family" in the email, trying to send it to me—the only word that meant the world to him. What we all did not realise was that he was pointing at the family picture with his fist closed, knowing that if he had opened it, the cufflink would have dropped out. He did not name you directly, so he was sending the next best clue to me. With mom gone, him shot, and the email addressed to me, you were the only one left. But life dwindled away before he could send it. Instead of deleting the email fully, you thought of a convenient scheme to lead the police astray. Connivingly, you deleted the last four letters and then fed us the baked story of them being the initials of someone. You then minimised it and let it be there. That was the only way to be sure the police would look at it.

The next step was to change your clothes before the police arrived. You could have been exposed to the blood splatter, or your father's prints, or some form of DNA could have come onto your clothes. The gloves you had on must have gotten gunpowder residue on them, for sure. You ran up to your room, being careful not to make any noise. While changing, you realised that the cufflink was torn out by your father in the scuffle and that it was still in his hand. You had to get it out of his hand immediately. You hid the clothes and the gun somewhere in the room and went downstairs. What you didn't take into account was Andy calling the police. He did not see you leave the study. But when he heard the shot, he knew something was wrong. He must have called out father's name from outside the room. He waited before entering the room, and when he saw his father lying in a pool of blood, he immediately called the police.

You came down and saw Andy in the study, standing next to father's dead body. You knew he would not leave the study now. You realised it was too late to take the cufflink out. Since Andy was standing in the study, panicking, and not moving, you had to do something else to get out of this predicament. Since you knew and kept track of everything happening in the mansion, you must have known there was an extra pair of cufflinks in his room. You quickly went up to his room, found the box, and, with your handkerchief, picked up one of the cufflinks from the box. You carefully wrapped it up, so as not to get your prints on it, and kept it in your pocket.

Next, you ran to the DVR room behind the study, being careful not to be spotted by Andy, who was still in the study and took out the drive of the camera in the study. You knew exactly which drive to take because you knew about the surveillance of the house. You erased the last few minutes of the footage on the other DVR and left the rest as it is. You had to give the police footage of Cliff and Paulo coming in to divert their attention and give them someone to investigate. The perfect motive, a wanted Don, and a partner with everything to gain. You then carefully and discreetly went to your room. Andy must have finally come to his senses and realised you were in the mansion as well. He came running to you for help. You then came downstairs and saw the body. Acting all shocked and trembling in front of Andy, you called me.

You were waiting for your moment to switch the cufflink, but Andy was with you the whole time. Then the police arrived, and they must have asked you and Andy to leave the room. The police would not let you near the body. Then you saw me come in and knew that with me you would be allowed to come close enough to make your move. You hugged me and stayed with me, crying about the incident. I think Andy also got a little suspicious and wanted to keep an eye out because he did not know for sure what happened. He quietly went behind the book rack to observe what was happening. That is why we found him behind the book rack when we came in.

When I finally made the mistake and took you near his body, you knew this was your best shot to get the cufflink out. The entire police force was here, and your own brother, the detective, was with you. Even if you touched the body, it would be dismissed just as easily with a warning. With so many witnesses, you acted swiftly and pulled the cufflink out while dropping the other one on the floor. You then turned around and wiped your tears with the same handkerchief."

"Are you done with this bullshit?" asked Darcy with both hands up. "You still have no proof the cufflinks were switched, Charles."

"Getting to it. You realised that Andy may eventually figure out what happened, but at the moment he was clueless, so you let him be and kept close watch. Father had realised the same thing: that you had been keeping a close watch on him through the cameras and that he was always under your surveillance. You had access to everything. So father decided to get extra security for his library, something that even you did not know about, just in case he required it, and he was right. He even got the walls soundproofed.

Now this is where Andy came into the picture. He had found the bill for the cufflinks and the installation of the security camera in the study. He tried to tell me about it, but you were always around. Andy kept two bills for me in the secret drawer, the only place, Darcy, you never knew about.

The bill of the cufflinks showed that father had ordered 25 pairs, i.e., 21 pairs of silver and 4 pairs of platinum. The captain had spoken to 20 people who had the cufflinks with them. Then the four of us had the platinum: you Darcy, me, father, and Cliff.

There was still one pair unaccounted for, the last pair that father had to give to someone. But what you did not know was that this was a silver one and not the platinum one. Father had them made to look exactly the same. The platinum ones are really strong compared to the silver ones. If father had ripped out a silver one from the killer's shirt, they would have broken easily. They could never rip the cuff of a shirt. I found this out when I asked Lisa to pull the cufflinks out the other evening while recreating the murder scene. They looked identical, so even Lisa did not realise that. I used one platinum cufflink, which I took from the pair my father gave me, and the other was silver, which we found at Cliff's. The silver one, like I guessed, broke, but the platinum one did not. They ripped the cuff a bit."

"So it wasn't inconclusive," said Lisa.

"Great, so now the cufflinks were switched by me, then where did the clothes and the gun go?" Darcy asked fuming.

"I'll get to the gun later. Well, you knew one thing: you could not just throw the shirt. It had to be disposed of properly. The barbecue was the answer to that. I saw black smoke on the terrace when I came. You were on the roof before us. That is when you burned the shirt and conveniently covered it with the excuse of having a barbecue. Since I was late that evening after talking to Cliff, assuming the fire was lit even half an hour ago, the smoke should not have been like that of a fresh fire. Rather, it should have been dripping by then. The food was already made when I came and on the table. Why was there so much smoke as if something had just been burned? Since we got late, you thought it was the best time to get cracking at your father's laptop to get access to his bank account. I realised it was not your laptop that you were working on. It was father's laptop, which is why you were not able to access it. That is why I asked you twice if you needed help. Realising I would keep asking, you immediately kept it behind you and acted normal.

The next day, news got out, and Paulo must have found out that father had been shot, and he had to recover his money from you now. So after a few days, when the funeral was held, Paulo sent back the killer. He came back to kill you since you were not paying back, and you killed the person capable of doing it."

"But the killer took a shot at you, Charles," said Lisa, "Not Darcy."

"I thought that too, but then I realised Darcy was standing right behind me and you and he was aiming for her. But he missed, and the bullet grazed you instead. He had shot from a good distance, behind the bushes. Thank your stars, he missed them. He then jumped the fence and fled. The next time, again, the killer followed us to the diner and waited for Darcy to come out, but she did not. So he decided to make his move. He wanted Darcy to see him from the window and react—maybe even follow him out—but instead, Lisa saw him, and I followed him. When he caught me, he had several occasions to shoot me, but he did not. This is what kept troubling me. Why would a trained shooter not kill me at such close range, even when he had the perfect chance? That's when I was convinced he was not there for me. I thought he kept mumbling something again and again. He was actually trying to communicate. He kept saying the word "audite," which is actually Latin. If translated to English, it means "listen". I thought he was just mumbling. Later, I looked it up on the internet. He wanted to say something, but in the heat of the moment, I did not pay attention to it. He wanted to tell me he was there for you, but could not due to the language barrier. You immediately recognised him because you must have seen him with Paulo when you met him for the money. That is why, when I signalled you for the gun instead of handing it to me, you shot him in the throat, the only way he would not talk even if caught. Once arrested, he would have eventually spoken to us. The next day, you were absolutely normal. You showed no remorse, as if you had done this before—no shock, no reaction. People take weeks and years to get out of this trauma and even require professional help. They have trouble even getting out of bed. That made me sure something wasn't right.

Coming back to Andy, he also realised something was wrong. I am guessing he found the camera behind the bookshelf, which was mentioned in the bill. You also knew something was not right with Andy—the way he was behaving—and wanted to confront him and get an idea of what he knew. He spoke to me about father's belongings and some documents in front of you. But we had to go to the police station for our statements. You got ready and waited for me and Darcy to step out first so that we could see you running to our car, as if you were a person who was late and in a genuine hurry. You planned and pre-recorded a fake call and made your phone ring just as you were about to get in the car—perfect timing. You made up the story of an accident to once and for all handle Andy. We had no reason to get suspicious. It was a genuine emergency. So we drove off to the station. At the station, Andy called me but hesitated to tell me about the camera on the phone. He wanted to do it in person because he realised you were always watching and always listening. He was right in his suspicion. You intercepted the call and heard him on the parallel line and feared that he had found the camera footage.

You definitely would have checked the camera yourself, just to be sure. You must have noticed that the memory card was gone. The logical explanation was that Andy took it out and was bringing it to me. So you decided to follow him and do something about it before he could reach me. On the U-bend at the midpoint of the valley, you decided to end it and rammed his car from behind, pushing it off the road into the valley. Being on a remote road with no surveillance, it was the best spot to do this. You knew this because you use that route to go to work every day. You then conveniently dropped off your car for repairs and came to the police station in a taxi.

Someone driving by later must have seen the accident and called it in while we were all at the station. Luck favoured you that day, as it happened after you reached it, keeping you completely out of suspicion. Then, when the accident was called in, you were quick to blame it on Cliff before we could think of any other angle. It was easy from there. Things were going exactly the way you wanted them to. We drove to his lodge. Once there, you pointed to his damaged car. While we were confronting Cliff, you went near the garage and threw the other silver cufflink in the bushes for the deputy to find. We saw the damaged car and were quick to judge Cliff, saying that it was him. What you did not know was that me and the captain both realised this was too easy and sudden, so we decided to play along, and we sent him to the station. He was actually taken back to protective custody. That is why I did not go to question him."

"That's it!" shouted Darcy furiously. She got up and pulled out the deputy's gun while standing next to her. "I have been hearing all this crap theory quietly, and now I cannot bear this anymore. It's just Charles's stories and theories. None of this is evidence-based. Just facts and facts. I swear, I am going to shoot Cliff myself. I know for sure he shot father."

Lisa and Cliff quickly got under the table to hide.

"Don't do that, Darcy. Let's all calm down and talk, please," Charles said, as Nate and the deputies pointed the gun at Darcy. "Hand over the gun quietly."

Darcy realised that this made her look more like a suspect and handed the gun back to the captain. She was then made to sit in the chair again, this time handcuffed.

"I am not going to ignore that, Darcy," said Nate in a stern and angry tone. "If I had just facts, do you think I would have ever asked for your arrest? You are like my sister and always will be. This is the most difficult thing I have had to do in my life."

Charles continued, "Coming back to the second bill Andy left me. I started looking for the camera and found it. The wire was loose on the floor, which suggested someone had already pulled on it. I saw the memory card was gone, so I decided to check Andy's clothes and car. I did not find the memory card, but I found something even better on the trunk: a scratch line of white paint. There were two sets of white paint, which meant there was another car there, and it was not an accident. One paint was old, the other seemed fresh. I scraped some off and sent it for testing at the lab. It must have been missed because the car toppled over many times. They must have mistaken it for a scratch. I knew there was a player in the background but could not stitch everything together. Then the other day, you told me that your car was leaking oil, and you sent it for repairs. Thank God that it was actually leaking. You were right. I did not see it because it had rained last night. But the good thing about oil is that it never gets out with just water, it's so slick.

I noticed when looking carefully that the oil had stuck to the pebbles on the driveway, and I picked a few of them up and bagged them. I then went to the site of Andy's crash and carefully examined the road. Just where the tyre tracks were, there was oil on the road. I scraped it out a bit and bagged it. I then carefully looked at the tyre marks and measured them. They did not match the width of the tyres Andy had on his car. I took a photo of his spares and had them measured by an expert at the station. I then came back home and measured your tyres. They were a match. Lisa's tyres were again narrow. I had all this cross-checked at the department just to be absolutely sure. I then called the captain for an analysis of the oil found. Captain, can you tell me if the oil on the stones matches?"

"Yes, they did, Charles."

"That means you were there, and when you hit Andy's car from the back, you drove it over the ledge. Your tyre tracks were grinding the road since he must have put his brakes on. Your broad tyre tracks covered his narrow ones, which is why only one set of tracks was found at the site. Since your car was white like Andy's, I got a little sceptical. I examined your car and found the paint on the entire car was new. It had been repainted fully. A car sent for an oil change gets repainted, that was new to me. I looked under the car and found some of the old paint, scraped it off, and bagged it. I again troubled the captain for an analysis. Captain, did the paint on Andy's car match the paint I scraped off Darcy's car or Cliff's car?"

"Yes, they matched, Charles. They matched Darcy's car."

"Before you get all riled up again, Darcy, I know this is not enough to put you away for Andy's murder attempt because you could say you scratched his car while parking it next to it in the mansion garage, so I needed something cogent to corroborate this find. What you forgot, Darcy, was your GPS history. Your car records it, and I copied it. It confirmed what I had been fearing all along. You were at the point of an accident.

Now comes the gun, which we still do not have. There was one other place where your car had stopped other than banks, malls, etc. The lake that you so much love. I am sure the gun is at the bottom of the lake. I gave the coordinates to the captain to send a search party. Captain, what did the search party find?"

"No luck there, Charles. They are still looking."

"So no murder weapon and no footage from the camera in the study or the secret camera?" Darcy started laughing.

Charles continued, "What if I told you I don't need the gun, Darcy?"

Darcy immediately stopped laughing and choked. "What do you mean?"

"Now this brings me back to the main point: the footage from the two cameras. First, the footage from the camera in the study must have been destroyed by now, so there is no point looking for that drive. It could even be with the gun at the bottom of the lake. Second, the footage from the hidden camera. It must have captured the shooter's face since the camera was right behind the father's table and would have recorded everything."

"So no footage and nothing to show I did it then, Charles. Still nothing?" said Darcy with a smirk. "You had me there for a second. Good one, brother."

"Well, that's the best part. Remember how our father used to play games with us, like indications and treasure hunts? You forgot that. You made the very mistake he asked us never to make. You stopped looking, you didn't try hard enough, and you forgot to empty your mind and think from a fresh perspective."

Charles turned around and walked to the other side of the table. "What if there never was a memory card?"

"What? That makes no sense. If there was no memory card, then why install the camera?" asked Darcy.

"Glad you asked. If you read the description on the bill, it is a plug-and-play WiFi camera that can be viewed from anywhere with an internet connection, and the footage can be recorded or backed up. Father was not technology-savvy, so he got it done through the agency. The software was installed somewhere since the agency had charged for 'installation' in the bill. I thought to myself, a simple plug-and-play camera, why would it require installation? I started looking for it on his computer but did not find it.

Then I saw your laptop in the study, on the side desk, and thought, Why would you leave it there? It was then that I saw father's initials on the laptop bag kept under it and realised it was his laptop you were trying to open the other night. You could access his office computer and his surveillance because you used it many times. This was given by the firm for official work, so he never shared the password with you, following his privacy principles. I took the laptop and asked the guys at the station to help out. They cracked the password. I smiled when they shared the password with me—another one of my father's games and secrets hiding in plain sight.

Guess what? He had it all backed up—the only place you could never get through because you could have never figured out his password."

He then took out his father's laptop from a bag and put it on the table. He turned it around. "I present to you my father's final piece of the puzzle from the grave."

He typed in the password, DARCY. The laptop opened. He browsed through the menu and found the camera software installed.

He played the footage, saying, "By the way, this also had audio, so that nothing is missed this time."

First, Paulo was seen coming in. Andy was seen serving tea.

"What brings you here?" asked Robert.

"It's your daughter, Darcy," Paulo replied in his Latin accent.

"Darcy? What does she have to do with your visit?"

"She owes me three million, and she has not paid back a penny. You saved me once, Robert. I am indebted to you. Therefore, I show this courtesy to you. Otherwise, you know what I am capable of and what I do to people who take my money."

Robert shouted at him with anger, "Don't you dare, Paulo, you thankless scum. Don't you dare threaten my daughter."

"I have come to talk, haven't I, Robert? I could have taken action first, you know."

"I will pay on her behalf, but you have to promise me that she will never see you again, and neither will I after this. This is the end of our relationship. Darcy must never know it has been done. I will transfer the money tomorrow. You will not touch one hair on her body, promise me."

Paulo agreed, and while walking out, he turned and said, "Like they say, attorney-client privilege, huh? This will stay between us." He left the mansion.

Then Cliff was seen coming in, and as he said, he just spoke of Robert being careful with Paulo and all and left. Robert told him not to worry because he knew Paulo would not be back after that day. Then Darcy entered the room in a dark coat and white shirt, wearing the cufflinks, as if she were just back from her office.

"What was Paulo here for, father?"

Robert shouted back, "I told you a thousand times to stop keeping an eye on me for everything. He is my client. Take care of your worthless business and devote time there."

"What did he say to you? He wanted me, didn't he? He wants to kill me. He told you about the money, didn't he?"

Robert got even more furious and starts shouting, "If you knew he would, then why do you get into all this shit, Darcy? Why can't you live a normal life? Why take the money from him?"

"There you go again, with your lectures. I know what I am doing. I did not ask you for more, but I had to take it from someone. The banks won't give me a penny more," Darcy shouted back. "I just need money to pay him back."

"More money!" shouted Robert. "You have lost millions, and still you want more. I will not give you even a penny more. Deal with this on your own. It's not your business that is a lost cause, it's you."

Charles paused the video and said, "This is the same gesture seen from the outside camera. What you see now is the whole picture."

He resumed the footage.

"I don't care. I need more. You are my father. You are obligated to take care of me no matter what."

"Didn't you hear me? Not a penny more. You have already taken everything. No more."

"You don't understand. If I don't pay back Paulo, he will kill me."

"Well, then so be it. Let him, but I won't pay more. Maybe you will finally learn the value of money."

Robert knew in his heart that he had already settled for her. No harm would come to her, but this was a good way to keep her spending in check. He turned around and went back to the computer table. Darcy took out the gun from her bag.

He was then seen getting up again and calmer. Darcy was pointing his own gun at him. "Give me the money. I am desperate, and I can't let him kill me. You have enough just to pay him off this last time. I really want to live. I am scared he will come for me."

"Where did you get that? My own blood pointed a gun at me. Lower that right now and give it back before things get out of hand. Alright, alright, I will give you the money," Robert waved his hand. "Just lower the gun."

Darcy does not lower it.

"I don't trust you. You are very good at games. You do it now, transfer it to this account, and I will lower the gun."

Darcy showed him an account number on her phone screen with the other hand, which could not be seen on the camera earlier.

"Fine, give me the phone, and I will note it down," said Robert, using it as an excuse to walk up to Darcy. Robert then swiftly, instead of the phone, grabbed the gun, and Darcy tried to pull back, but when she did, her cufflink got ripped off and the trigger got squeezed. They both stood still and suddenly Robert stumbled. He held his chest and slowly turned around. Robert was seen walking back to the table. Robert passed away.

Charles paused the video.

"Darcy, do you still have someone to blame?"

Darcy started to cry.

"I didn't mean to," she said, sobbing. She looked up. "I didn't mean to do it. I just wanted to scare him into giving me the money. He had millions of it. He could have saved me, but he refused. I just wanted the money and nothing more. If I knew he had settled for me already, it would have never come to this. I never wanted to pull the trigger. It got squeezed in the scuffle. You have to trust me, Charles. Please trust me on this."

"Well, what's done is done. The consequences will follow," said Charles as tears came down his cheeks.

He turned to the captain and said, "Captain, please take care of her. She has done wrong, but she is my sister. I cannot bring myself to arrest her."

The captain nodded in agreement, got up, and placed Darcy under arrest while reading her rights. They all walked out of the mansion, except Lisa and Charles. As soon as they walked out and put Darcy in the back of the police car, Charles, looking from the window inside, could not control himself any longer. He started crying and howling as loud as he could. He kept crying. Lisa tried her best but was unable to pacify him. Lisa got up and got him some water, but he was inconsolable. "I lost my entire family in weeks," he kept crying. "Miss you, mom and dad."

"Drink this, please. I know nothing seems well right now, but all is over now. At least you have closure."

"My own family, Lisa, is gone and destroyed—one killed, one in the hospital, and one in jail—all because of money and nothing more. No anger, no regrets, no animosity, no revenge—nothing, just money. The funny bit is that the money is also missing. No one knew about it yet fought and killed for it."

"Well, Charles, that is life for you. It pulls out all the stops to astonish you, and money gets people to do things they regret later. Even family ties get blurred."

"I feel like being alone now. Is that okay?"

"Yes, that's fine."

Charles started climbing the stairs to go up to his room. He slammed the door behind him. He was seen crying, sitting next to the bed.

Chapter 13

The Money

A few weeks passed by, and Charles did not come out of his room much, sitting there drinking and sulking in his thoughts. Lisa took care of him. He ate in the room, drank till he passed out, and did not respond to any calls. Days and weeks kept passing by, but he just drifted along.

One day, Charles was in bed, lying on his stomach with one arm hanging from the bed, looking out the window and around the room. His gaze fell upon the book left for him by Andy, the one his father had left for him. For some unknown reason, he felt the urge to read this book. He picked himself up and dragged his body out of bed to pick up that book and read it. What was so special about this little thing anyway that his father left it to Andy?

He opened the book, and it seemed pretty normal to him—a simple novel. He flipped the pages, but there was nothing new there either. He decided to read the book, a fairly small one and reached the end. At the end of the book, he noticed there were three stars in a triangular form. He looked around for the publisher's symbol on the book, but it was behind the book on the rim and was completely different. The back of the book seemed a little heavy and as if it had been pasted back together. Charles ripped the side of the book, and it had a small cavity and a thick sheet of paper with squares cut out. It was kind of a stencil, and there was a USB drive in it.

He got up in astonishment and looked for his laptop. He stumbled around and found it in his desk drawer. He picked it up and plugged in the USB. He was surprised to see a recording of Robert sitting. Charles' eyes teared up as he hit play.

"Hello, son, if you are seeing this, then you have proved what I knew all along. You are the best at what you do, and as you may have realised, I am dead. Otherwise, this book would have never come to you. I recorded this video because I knew my life was in danger and I had to get the money out. I was always under surveillance and always being watched, but I managed to transfer it out. I have no way to know for sure if you are seeing this, Charles, or if someone else has found it." Robert paused and winked. "Listen carefully now. I always told you from the start that when you want to think, clear your mind completely. Empty space will always have the answers. Miss me, my dear boy, and remember, your father always loved you till his last breath. Family is everything, take care of them, even if they stumble or fail. Treasure my writings always. Someday, we will meet again. Goodbye."

The video ended.

The USB contained this video and another empty folder on the drive, but it had nothing in it. Charles could not make heads or tails of it.

Lisa entered the room. "Hey, it's nice to see you out of bed today. How are you feeling?"

"Look, Lisa, my father left me a message, but I cannot understand what he is trying to tell me. It's all coded."

She watched the video, which made no sense to her except for the plain language and the message conveyed. But she also knew that, with Robert, nothing was simple.

"Charles, think of the lines that Robert kept repeating to you—his favourite ones during your childhood."

Charles thought for a while and identified the first one: "Empty space. He kept saying, *Clear your head. Empty space has all the answers.*"

Lisa decided to give it a try. Using her strong background in computers, she tried to analyse the USB drive. There was just a video and an empty folder in it. She looked for hidden files, but there was nothing there. She watched the video again and mumbled, "What other empty space could he be talking about?"

She noted the size of the video file and the folder and subtracted it from the total available space on the drive. "That's odd. There should be more space available. Some extra space is missing. But there are no hidden files either, and no system files."

"Is there some other way to find out? I don't want to take it to the guys at the station."

"Hold on, let me try something," said Lisa. She downloaded and ran the software. That did the trick. The software showed that there was a hidden drive within the drive, a small file that could not be detected easily.

The file, when opened, just had some numbers on it. Charles noted them down. He and Lisa played the video again and again, trying to pick up the next hint. Robert was talking in indications, they understood the pattern. It was like a verbal anagram. Charles was not able to get them. They deciphered the first one and were stuck now.

Watching it on repeat, he suddenly jolted up and realised the letters his father had sent him over the years were the treasures he spoke of in the video.

"What happened?" asked Lisa.

"I will be right back. Stay here. I'm sure it's worth a try."

He ran out of the mansion to his car. The letters were in his apartment in the city. Lisa shouted from behind, "Where are you going?" Charles did not respond and drove off. He reached his apartment and started looking for the box. He found it in storage above the closet. He pulled them out and started reading them. He did not see anything unusual about them. Sad and low, he took the box back to the mansion.

"Are you going to tell me what you are up to?" Lisa stomped on him and stopped him from entering. He kissed her on the cheek and said, "I will when I figure it out." He ran up to his room, and she followed.

"There has to be something in these letters. I know it for sure."

In the room, he spread the letters on the table and started looking at all of them for hidden clues. He picked one of them up and took it to the window for a better view of the paper. The sunlight made the paper translucent when held up against the window. He smiled. The letters had the same three-star symbol watermarked into the paper.

"It's the same as the stencil," He sprinted back to the table.

He then looked for the stencil and placed it on one of the letters. The stencil showed a few letters and hid the rest of the letters.

"But where do I start?"

"Maybe datewise?" said Lisa.

Charles put all the letters in date order and started covering them one by one with the stencil. He then started noting the letters on a pad. Charles smiled because he had figured out his father's hints and indications. The message started to decipher. Lisa watched all of this in silence.

Charles finished and called Lisa to see.

Lisa saw the message, and while hugging, they both started jumping around.

"We did it. If I am right, we found the money."

"But out of the blue, how did you suddenly find out, Charles? This morning, you were all depressed and sad."

He then sat her down and showed her. "Look, father left me the final piece of the mystery in this book, the one he left for Andy. He left the book to him, knowing he was the only one who could be trusted blindly, and no one would be curious if a single book was given to a butler out of an entire library. Plus, he had asked him to stay at the mansion till he was alive. Therefore, the book would have been in the mansion at all times and in the safe custody of Andy.

I picked up the book out of sheer curiosity and read it. The back cover of the book seemed oddly heavy. On the back cover of the book, there was this stencil and a drive with this video, which you saw. He left indications and not a clear message, just in case someone else finds the video. He said the empty space has the answers and that he should keep his treasures safe. We found the empty space, and the next step was finding the treasures.

His letters, he called them treasures, always, and said you will value them when I am gone. Well, the empty space on the drive had these numbers in it, and the letters sent to me when arranged give out this message. What I have to guess now is what they mean."

"Show me the numbers, Charles," she said. "Don't they look like coordinates?

"Latitude and longitude? No, they are longer by number each. Maybe it's a safe combination."

"Not quite right. See the zeros at the end of each number. What if they are degrees and not numbers? The symbols are the same for degree and zero, just the size difference."

Charles looked at them and realised she was right. "You are a genius. How did I miss this?"

He picked up the laptop and put in the numbers on the internet. They were indeed coordinates, and they pointed to the location of a bank in the Cayman Islands.

Charles looked at Lisa with a big smile and said, "You know what that means, don't you? We are going on a vacation."

"But what about the letters and the message decoded with the stencil?" asked Lisa. "It's just more letters and numbers, see?"

"Well, I could not figure out these numbers, but you did it. They were coordinates, so this leaves us with what is on the letter. The number in the letter looks like the account number. It is in between the two sets of letters. The first one looks like a name. If my guess is right, it's a made-up name that father used so that it does not get traced back to him. The last one, I am guessing, is another password to access the funds."

"Well, there is only one way to find out, isn't there? We are going to the Cayman Islands," jumped Lisa.

They both booked the flights and reached there the day after. They put in the coordinates and found out that it led to an empty parking spot.

"Damned, dead end again," said Lisa.

"No, don't dismiss things so easily. It's never easy solving his mysteries."

Charles started to walk around the parking area. There were a few cars parked, but nothing unique. In one of the corners, he saw a yellow painted stone. On it were the words, "due north."

He called Lisa and asked her to take out the compass on her phone. They pointed it to the north and started walking.

"Where are we going, Charles?"

"Trust me on this."

They kept walking and eventually reached a fairly large building.

"It's the bank," said Lisa.

"I told you it's never simple with father."

They went in and were greeted by the manager.

"Good day," he said with an accent. "What brings you to our bank?"

"We would like to access our account, please," replied Charles.

"Certainly, please follow me."

He stopped at the entrance of a room. "I am afraid you can only go beyond that. If you have an account name, please enter it on this terminal, and then you can enter further."

Charles entered his father's alias on the terminal and pressed enter. The door opened.

"Please use the computer in the room to enter your account number and to transfer funds."

The manager then walked away, giving them their privacy. Lisa and Charles went in and found the computer. On the screen, it had just two fields: account number and password.

Charles said to Lisa, "Are you ready for this?"

Lisa got all excited and said, "I can't wait a second longer. Go for it."

Charles entered the username and password and pressed enter. Nothing happened. Then the message flashed, "receiving". Charles and Lisa were both holding hands and, in anticipation, trying to hold on to their excitement.

Suddenly, numbers like entries start rolling, and then they stop at the total. Seeing that, Charles and Lisa almost fainted. They looked at each other again in disbelief, and Charles started counting the zeros.

"Gosh, Darcy could not have been more wrong when she said he had millions. She didn't have the slightest indication that he had billions."

Lisa had no words. She just nodded.

The account balance showed three billion dollars and two options below: transfer to account and cash out. Charles cashed out 10,000 dollars. The machine made some computing noises, and the ATM behind them, within the room, dispensed the cash. The balance was updated on the screen. They were flabbergasted. They walked out of the room with the money.

Outside, the manager was waiting for them. He stopped them. They got a bit worried. "We hope you liked our services, and we hope you understand that discretion and secrecy are of utmost importance to us, Mr. Charles. The only reason you were even allowed inside was because Robert allowed it."

"How did you know who I am?"

"Well, when your father had the money sent to us, he said he might not come, but one day his son might. He sent us your photos, your biodata, your fingerprints, and even your DNA. We have to be thorough before we allow anyone in. Our system scanned you the moment you entered it and approved it. He asked us to be okay with that and let you use his account. You are the joint account holder. I require your signatures on these transfer papers, and the money is all yours."

Charles signed them.

"Here is a mobile to access our bank from anywhere in the world. You can transfer the money to any account you choose. If you get into trouble with the authorities, break the phone, and no one can trace the money. Call this number from anywhere and say, 'My machine needs repairs, the motor is dead.' We will send you a new phone at the address you state on the call. It will be sealed inside the empty shell of the spare motor. Everything we do is a mirage, and that is how we like it to be. I hope you understand all of this."

"Yes, I do."

The manager's assistant whispered something in his ear.

"One last thing, I have just been informed that Robert had also asked us to give you this pen drive if ever you came instead of him. I never thought this day would come, so I never bothered about the contents of it. We all know how Robert was. Even if I tried, it would have been futile. I could never break that man's codes. Finally, I repeat myself before going: secrecy and discretion."

The manager handed over the pen drive and left.

"What do you think is on this drive now, Charles?"

"Well, there's only one way to find out."

They both walk out the door with a big grin on their faces.

The End